"No! Stop!"

The wall of lockers on her left swung open in unison, then slammed shut with a deafening crash.

"No! Please!"

She held her hands over her ears and ran.

And then she heard the screams.

A girl, screaming in horror.

High-pitched, shrill screams of anguish, of pain . . .

Bobbi's sneakers pounded against the floor. She ran blindly through the dark hallway, locker doors swinging open, then slamming shut on both sides of her.

Another scream of agony.

Bobbi reached the end of the corridor, turned the corner, and stared in surprise. . . .

Books by R. L. Stine

HOW I BROKE UP WITH
  ERNIE
PHONE CALLS
CURTAINS
BROKEN DATE

Fear Street Cheerleaders

THE FIRST EVIL
THE SECOND EVIL
THE THIRD EVIL

Fear Street Super Chiller

PARTY SUMMER
SILENT NIGHT
GOODNIGHT KISS
BROKEN HEARTS

Fear Street

THE NEW GIRL
THE SURPRISE PARTY
THE OVERNIGHT
MISSING
THE WRONG NUMBER
THE SLEEPWALKER
HAUNTED
HALLOWEEN PARTY
THE STEPSISTER
SKI WEEKEND
THE FIRE GAME
LIGHTS OUT
THE SECRET BEDROOM
THE KNIFE
PROM QUEEN
FIRST DATE
THE BEST FRIEND
THE CHEATER
SUNBURN

Available from ARCHWAY Paperbacks

FEAR STREET®
R·L·STINE

CHEERLEADERS
The First Evil

AN ARCHWAY PAPERBACK
Published by POCKET BOOKS
New York   London   Toronto   Sydney   Tokyo   Singapore

This book is a work of fiction. Names, characters, places and incidents are either products of the author's imagination or are used fictitiously. Any resemblance to actual events or locales or persons, living or dead, is entirely coincidental.

AN ARCHWAY PAPERBACK *Original*

An Archway Paperback published by
POCKET BOOKS, a division of Simon & Schuster Inc.
1230 Avenue of the Americas, New York, NY 10020

ISBN: 0-671-75117-4

First Archway Paperback printing August 1992

10 9 8 7 6

FEAR STREET is a registered trademark of Parachute Press, Inc.

AN ARCHWAY PAPERBACK and colophon are registered trademarks of Simon & Schuster Inc.

Cover art by Edwin Herder

Printed in the U.S.A.

IL 7+

PART ONE

The Cheers

Chapter 1

The Evil Sister

"**Y**ou are evil," Corky said in a hushed whisper. "You are truly evil."

The words made Bobbi grin, her green eyes lighting up with pleasure. She gripped the rat tighter around its rib cage.

"Where are you going to put it?" Corky asked, still rubbing the sleep from her eyes. The floorboards felt cold beneath her bare feet. "Right in front of Sean's door?"

Bobbi nodded and tiptoed down the narrow hall toward their brother's room. Her blond hair was still tangled from sleep. Both girls were in long, cotton nightshirts.

"Sean is terrified of rats," Corky whispered, her eyes on her little brother's door, expecting him to burst out and ruin Bobbi's little surprise.

"I know," Bobbi said with an evil snicker. She carefully set the rat down in the center of the doorway. When Sean came out for breakfast, he'd have to walk right into it.

"It looks so real," Corky whispered. "It doesn't look like rubber." The floor creaked noisily and Corky stopped. She set one hand against the peeling wallpaper and leaned on it.

"It's the hair that makes it," Bobbi replied. Having set down the realistic-looking creature, she and her sister started to back away, their eyes on Sean's closed door. "It's very good rat hair. Very authentic."

"Girls? What are you doing?" Their mother's voice interrupted them from downstairs, startling them both. "Are you dressed yet? You're going to be late. Come down for breakfast. And make sure Sean is up."

"Don't worry," Bobbi whispered, grinning at her sister, "Sean will be wide-awake real soon!"

Chuckling about Bobbi's little joke, both girls descended the creaking staircase and joined their parents in the kitchen. Mr. Corcoran, their handsome, young-looking father, was already at the table, wiping egg off his chin with a paper napkin.

"Yuck. Not poached eggs again," Bobbi groaned.

Mrs. Corcoran turned around, a pale reflection of her vibrant, blond daughters. She stared at their nightshirts, frowning. "That's how you're going to school?"

"Yeah," Bobbi answered quickly. "All the girls are wearing nightshirts. It's sort of a trend."

"Why do we have to have poached eggs?" Corky asked, pouring herself a half glass of orange juice.

"You need a lot of energy," their mother replied, dumping two runny eggs on two pieces of toast with a plastic spatula.

Mr. Corcoran yawned loudly. "I don't sleep well in this house."

"No one does," Corky muttered, taking her place at the breakfast table. The two eggs on her plate stared up at her like giant, runny eyes. "It's the ghosts."

"Yeah. This place is definitely haunted," Bobbi quickly agreed.

"Haunted? That's ridiculous." Mrs. Corcoran set down a plate in front of Bobbi, who made a disgusted face.

"This girl I met at school—Lisa Blume—she told me that *all* the houses on Fear Street are haunted," Corky said, poking her eggs with her fork, watching the yellow run over the toast.

"Just because a house is old and creaky it doesn't mean it's haunted," Mr. Corcoran replied.

"I think someone was murdered in my room," Bobbi said, glancing across the table at her sister. Bobbi was the one with the wild imagination. "Someone keeps whispering to me late at night, whispering and crying."

"Probably the wind," their father said, straightening his tie with one hand and taking a sip from his coffee cup with the other.

"Yeah, sure. The wind," Bobbi said sarcastically.

Sitting across from each other, Corky and Bobbi looked like twins, even though Bobbi was a year older. Both had blond hair, very light, very fine, which they wore brushed straight to their shoulders or sometimes in ponytails or single braids. Both had lively green eyes, creamy, pale skin, and high cheekbones like models.

Bobbi was seventeen but nearly two inches shorter than her younger sister, which annoyed her no end. Corky, on the other hand, was envious of her sister's figure. Corky was tall but boyish. Sometimes she felt gawky and wished she'd hurry up and fill out.

"Well, your brother is certainly not having any trouble sleeping in this house," Mrs. Corcoran said, heading toward the front stairs. "Didn't you wake him up?"

They heard a deafening scream, a hideous scream of terror from upstairs. Sean had obviously discovered the rat.

"I think he's up," Bobbi said dryly.

Both girls collapsed in laughter, lowering their heads to the table.

"What did you two do?" Mrs. Corcoran demanded. She hurried to the rescue.

"We didn't do it! The ghost did it!" Bobbi called after her.

Mr. Corcoran simply shook his head. He was used to having his daughters play tricks on Sean. They loved to take advantage of their brother's trusting personality.

Taking another sip of coffee, Mr. Corcoran sighed, wondering what hideous thing they had just done to make poor Sean scream like that.

The girls were still snickering when Sean entered the kitchen, fully dressed in faded jeans and a red Gap T-shirt, swinging the rat by the tail. "It didn't fool me at all," he told his sisters.

"You always scream like that when you get up, right?" Bobbi teased.

"I just did that so you wouldn't be disappointed," Sean said, avoiding their eyes.

Mrs. Corcoran followed him into the kitchen and rested her hands on his slender shoulders. "This house is creepy enough," she scolded the girls. "Do we really need *rats?*"

Sean set the rat down on the breakfast table. Mrs. Corcoran quickly grabbed it away. "Not on the table. Please!"

"It's not as disgusting as these eggs," Bobbi griped.

Sean glanced from one plate to another. "Looks like rat puke."

"Sean—*please!*" his mother exclaimed.

"Another delightful Corcoran family breakfast," their father said, pulling himself up and scraping his chair noisily back along the faded, old linoleum.

"Have your breakfast," Mrs. Corcoran told the girls, glancing at the clock. "Don't you have cheerleader tryouts this afternoon?"

"If they'll let us try out," Corky said glumly. The light in her emerald eyes faded. "The squad is already full. They say they picked everyone last spring. Before we moved here."

"But you girls are the best!" their mother declared, plopping two eggs onto a plate for Sean. "You were both all-state back home in Missouri. You practically took your squad to the national championships."

"You both stink," Sean said flatly.

"No one asked your opinion," Mr. Corcoran told Sean. "Hey—I'm outta here." He gave his wife a quick kiss on the cheek and disappeared out the

7

kitchen door. "Good luck this afternoon, girls!" they heard him call from outside.

"We'll need it," Corky muttered.

"When you jump up, everyone can see your underpants," Sean said nastily.

"Sean—eat your eggs," Mrs. Corcoran replied sharply. She pushed the plate closer to him, then glanced down at the girls, concern wrinkling her pale face. "They *should* let you try out at least. When they see how good you are—"

"Miss Green said it was up to the girls on the squad," Corky said.

"Who's Miss Green? The advisor?" their mother asked, pouring herself a cup of coffee.

"Yeah. We met her and we met the squad captain—Jennifer something-or-other," Bobbi said. "She seemed really nice."

"So they'll let you try out?" Mrs. Corcoran asked, motioning for Sean to eat faster.

"Maybe," Corky said doubtfully.

"We'll see after school," Bobbi said. She took a final bite of toast, pushed her chair back, and hurried upstairs to get dressed.

"You two could put Shadyside High on the map," Mrs. Corcoran yelled after her.

Corky laughed. "Mom, if it were up to you, we'd have it made."

"But you stink," Sean said quietly. Then he opened his mouth wide so Corky could see the yellow egg inside.

"You're gross," Corky said, frowning.

"You stink," he replied. It seemed to be the refrain of the morning.

"Knock it off," their mother scolded, rolling her eyes. "Hurry. Get dressed. You're all going to be late."

Corky took a last sip of orange juice, then headed upstairs, trying to decide what to wear. The kids at Shadyside were a lot more into clothes than her friends back in Missouri. She had the feeling that she'd need some new things, some short skirts, some tights, some leggings.

"Oh!"

She stopped on the landing and stared up at the hall railing. It took her a while to realize that she was staring at her sister.

"Bobbi!" she called.

Bobbi was dangling over the wooden railing, motionless, her arms hanging down. Her eyes were wide open in an unseeing stare, her mouth twisted in a wide O of horror.

"Bobbi!" Corky repeated, calling in a shrill voice she didn't recognize. "Bobbi!"

But her sister didn't move. Didn't blink.

Didn't breathe.

Chapter 2

Nervous Time

"Bobbi!"

Her heart in her throat, Corky lurched up the final stairs to her sister.

Bobbi raised her head, blinked, and an amused smile formed on her face. "Gotcha," she said softly. Pushing with both hands against the railing, she raised herself to a standing position.

"Bobbi—you rat!" Corky cried, her heart still thudding.

"You weren't supposed to find me," Bobbi said, still grinning delightedly that her little joke had worked so well. "Sean was supposed to come upstairs first."

"Don't ever do that again!" Corky cried, giving her sister a playful but hard punch on the shoulder. "You *know* I'm nervous about this house and trying out for cheerleading and everything."

"Nervous?" said Bobbi, following her sister into the room they shared. "Come on, Cork—lighten up. I mean, what's there to be nervous about?"

Her friends at Shadyside High were always telling Jennifer Daly that she looked like the movie star Julia Roberts. In fact, Jennifer did have the actress's large, dark eyes and sensual full lips. She was also tall and slender and moved with an easy grace.

A friendly girl with a soft voice and high, tinkling laugh, Jennifer had been the popular choice for captain of the Shadyside High Tigers cheerleading squad. She and Kimmy Bass, the squad's energetic assistant captain, had been good friends since elementary school. But Jennifer also got along well with the other cheerleaders. She was so easy to know and to like, and as Kimmy put it, "She isn't stuck up about anything."

Kimmy buzzed around Jennifer like a frenetic bumblebee. With her round face topped by a mop of crimped black hair, her full cheeks that always seemed to be pink, and her slightly chunky shape, she proved a striking contrast to her friend.

Their personalities were quite different too. While Jennifer was soft-spoken, serene, and graceful, Kimmy was loud, enthusiastic, and so full of energy that she seemed unable to stand still.

Standing under the basketball backboard, Jennifer straightened her T-shirt over her gray sweatpants and waited for the other members of the squad to enter the gym. She glanced up at the big clock next to the scoreboard. Three-twenty. School had just let out. Time for cheerleading practice to begin.

Kimmy was the next to arrive, the swinging double doors banging behind her as she hurried across the gym floor, waving to Jennifer. The bright overhead lights gave Kimmy's face a greenish tinge, Jennifer noticed. And as Kimmy drew closer, Jennifer saw that she had tiny beads of perspiration above her upper lip, a sure sign that Kimmy was worked up about something.

Jennifer didn't have to guess what Kimmy was upset about. It had to be the two Corcoran sisters, who, Jennifer noticed, had slipped into the gym and were huddled together on the far side of the floor near a section of wooden bleachers that had been lowered during the last gym class.

"I just don't think it's right!" Kimmy exclaimed, tossing her backpack to the floor, her round cheeks pink with excitement. "We already have our squad, Jennifer. We've practiced all summer. They can't just barge in. I don't care who they are!"

Jennifer closed her eyes briefly. Evidently Kimmy didn't realize how far her voice could travel in the big, empty gym. Or perhaps she didn't care. But she was talking loudly enough for the Corcoran sisters to overhear every word.

"Sshh," Jennifer whispered, gesturing with her eyes to the bleachers.

Kimmy turned quickly, following Jennifer's gaze. "I don't care," she repeated just as loudly as before. She shook her mop of hair, as if shaking away Jennifer's warning. "We can't let them try out, Jen. We can't. It just isn't fair."

The other cheerleaders were filing into the gym now, dropping their books and backpacks beside the wall, greeting one another in low tones, leaning against the tile wall to stretch out. Kimmy's friend Debra Kern entered and gave Kimmy a quick wave. She was followed by Heather Diehl and Megan Carman, who were best friends and always together. Entering last was Veronica (Ronnie) Mitchell, the only freshman to make the squad.

"Kimmy—they can *hear* you!" Jennifer repeated, embarrassed. She turned to the bleachers, where the Corcorans were now sitting side by side on the bottom bench, their hands clasped tensely in their laps. "You know, they're supposed to be terrific cheerleaders."

"Says who?" Kimmy snapped, crossing her arms in front of her chest.

"They were all-state back in their old hometown," Jennifer told her. "And you know that cheerleading competition that's on ESPN every year?"

"Yeah. We watched it together, remember?" Kimmy said almost grudgingly.

"Well, their cheerleading team won it last year. That's how good the Corcorans are."

"But who cares, Jen?" Kimmy cried emotionally, uncrossing her arms and gesturing with her hands. "We have a *great* team, don't we? We work together so well. We've practiced together for so long and—"

"But maybe they can make our team even better," Jennifer said, refusing to raise her voice. "After all, we want the very best girls we can get, don't we? I mean, maybe *we* could be all-state this year. Or be on ESPN or something."

"I agree with Kimmy," Debra broke in, stepping up beside her friend. She was beautiful but cold looking, with straight blond hair cut very short and icy blue eyes. Debra was an unlikely cheerleader. Short and thin, almost too thin, she seldom smiled. The only time she ever really seemed to come alive was when she was performing a cheer or a routine.

"Look at them," Jennifer said softly, turning her eyes to Corky and Bobbi. "They're here. We can at least let them do their stuff, don't you think? It won't hurt to watch them."

"But we had tryouts last spring," Kimmy insisted.

"Yeah," Debra chimed in. "We can't hold tryouts every week, you know." She fixed Jennifer with an icy stare.

"Is this a cheerleading squad or a debating team?" a harsh voice rang out loudly.

All of the cheerleaders turned to see Miss Green, their advisor, step quickly from her small office in the corner and move toward them with long, quick strides. Dressed in tight white tennis shorts, a gray short-sleeved T-shirt, and black high-tops, Miss Green was a compact woman with frizzy brown hair, a plain face that naturally seemed to fall into an angry expression, and a husky voice that always sounded as if she had a bad case of laryngitis.

She taught health and phys. ed., and had a reputation for being tough—a well-deserved reputation.

"We have three new routines to learn by Friday night," she called out loudly, her voice echoing off the tile walls of the vast gym. "So what's holding things up? Or have you learned the new routines already?"

"We're trying to decide about *them,*" Kimmy said, glancing first at Jennifer, then pointing to the Corcoran sisters, who had climbed to their feet.

14

"It's up to Jennifer," Miss Green said, staring at Jennifer. "The captain decides."

Kimmy, obviously miffed, made a face.

"I'd like to see what they can do," Jennifer said, staring defiantly at Kimmy. "I really think we should give them a chance."

"Okay. End of debate," Miss Green said brusquely. She waved to Corky and Bobbi. "Okay, you two!" she shouted. "You're on!"

"I don't believe this," Kimmy muttered darkly to Debra as they went to join the other girls against the wall. They stood beside Ronnie, and the three girls whispered among themselves, their expressions unhappy, as Corky and Bobbi made their way across the gym.

"Are you nervous?" Corky whispered to Bobbi, her eyes on the cheerleaders huddled against the wall.

"Who? *Me?*" Bobbi replied with a peal of nervous laughter. "Hey, come on. Why should *we* be nervous, Cork? We know we're good!"

"Tell that to my shaking knees!" Corky exclaimed.

Their sneakers squeaked as they hurried across the gleaming wood floor. The gym suddenly grew silent. The air felt heavy and hot.

"Show us whatever you like," Jennifer told them, flashing them an encouraging smile.

Corky and Bobbi each took a deep breath, glanced at each other for luck, stepped to the center of the floor, and huddled together.

"What should we do first?" Corky asked her older sister.

"Let's start with some synchronized walkovers,"

Bobbi suggested. "Then let's show them our double cartwheel."

"Why are they staring at us like that?" Corky asked, glancing over Bobbi's shoulder at the silent cheerleaders. "Like they hate us or something."

"Let's give them something to stare at," Bobbi replied, grinning.

"Break a leg," Corky said.

Chapter 3

First Scream

"Ohh!"

The cry from one of the cheerleaders told Bobbi that her spread eagle was as spectacular as she had planned.

Up, up, she leapt until she felt as if she could take off and fly. And then she shot out both legs, raising them up until they were perfectly straight. And then in her most startling move, Bobbi kept her legs outstretched as she gracefully floated down, hands high above her head like a diving bird, into a perfect split.

Then, before her stunned audience had recovered, she and Corky were into a powerhouse chant:

> *"First and ten,*
> *Do it again!*
> *First and ten,*
> *Do it again!*
> *Go Tigers!"*

It's going okay, Bobbi thought. At least they're not glaring at us anymore.

She glanced at her sister, gave her a quick nod, their signal for their big finish, and jumped.

Onto Corky's back. A perfect pony mount.

Then one swift move. Up. Arms up. And up again. Into the shoulder stand they had practiced day after day until their shoulders and backs were red and sore.

Good, Bobbi thought, standing straight and tall on Corky's shoulders, feeling Corky's hot hands lock onto the back of her legs. She smiled confidently, hands on hips. Then, without losing her smile, she suddenly dived off Corky's shoulders.

The cheerleaders gasped as she plummeted straight out. She completed a perfect flip and landed, standing on both feet. And then the sisters moved into a repeat of their double cartwheel. Corky grasped Bobbi's ankles as Bobbi grasped Corky's ankles, and the two girls rolled across the floor. They stood up with a final shout: "Go Tigers!"

The two sisters ran off clapping. Bobbi smiled at Corky as they leaned against the wall, catching their breath.

"Wow! They're incredible!" she heard one of the cheerleaders exclaim.

"How'd they do that?" she heard another ask in a loud whisper.

"You're putting on weight," Corky grumbled, rubbing her shoulders.

"Wow, that was great!" Jennifer said, smiling warmly, her dark eyes lighting up with genuine excitement.

"Thanks," Corky and Bobbi said in unison, smiling back at her.

They were standing awkwardly in Miss Green's office, a small glassed-in enclosure in the corner of the gym. Seated at the wooden desk, Miss Green was searching the top drawer for some forms.

The routine had been one of their best ever, Bobbi thought. Sometimes she and Corky just clicked, and that day had been one of those days.

All of the cheerleaders had been really excited and impressed. Except for the one named Kimmy and her short, blond friend. They had remained stone-faced, even when all the other girls had burst into appreciative applause.

"That was fabulous!" Miss Green had called out in her husky voice. "Of course your shoulder dive is impressive, but I also liked the height you got on those spread eagles." She turned to the squad members along the wall. "I'd like to see everyone work on the new routines, now. I hope Bobbi and Corky have inspired you to keep your energy up. Up!"

"Let's go!" Kimmy had yelled, clapping and running past Corky and Bobbi, avoiding their eyes as she led the squad to the center of the floor.

As the girls started to chant one of their new cheers, the two sisters had followed Jennifer and Miss Green into the corner office.

Jennifer motioned for the sisters to sit down on the folding chairs against the wall. Corky glanced quickly at Bobbi as they sat, a questioning glance.

"Do you mean we made the squad?" Bobbi asked Jennifer.

"Ah, here they are," Miss Green interrupted before Jennifer could reply. "You'll need to fill out these forms. This one's a health form," she said, pulling out a green sheet of paper. "And this one is the release form. Your parents have to sign that one."

"We made the squad?" Bobbi repeated, to Jennifer.

"Yeah. You were amazing!" Jennifer gushed. Then she added: "I used to be the star around here. But no one's going to notice me with you two around."

Bobbi couldn't decide if she was kidding or not. The girls reacted with embarrassed laughter. "We'll show you how to do the shoulder dismount," Bobbi offered.

"I think we can all learn something from you two," Miss Green added, shuffling through the sheaf of forms.

Jennifer's eyes flared just then, and Bobbi suddenly felt uncomfortable. Jennifer was making it clear that she was jealous of the Corcorans.

"Where did you get that double cartwheel thing after the dive?" Jennifer asked, leaning back against the yellow-tiled wall.

"We sort of made it up," Corky told her.

"Some other girls were doing something like it at the state finals back in Missouri last year," Bobbi added, "and we kind of adapted it."

"I hope *we* can get to the state finals," Jennifer said wistfully.

"With these two on the squad, it's a lock," Miss Green said, smiling one of her rare smiles as she handed the forms to Corky and Bobbi. As she stared at the girls, her expression changed to one of concern.

"Uniforms. Uniforms," she muttered. "This might be a problem. Quick." She pulled a pad of paper from her top drawer. "Write down your sizes. This will have to be a rush order."

A short while later Bobbi and Corky were thanking Jennifer and Miss Green; with the chants of their fellow cheerleaders ringing through the gym, they hurried out of the building, eager to congratulate each other.

Jennifer and Miss Green continued to confer over the low wooden desk, their expressions serious, concerned. Miss Green spoke heatedly, her eyes turning occasionally to watch the practice on the other side of the glass partition.

"The squad is supposed to be six," she told Jennifer. "I suppose we can squeeze one more girl on. But not two. We don't have the funds for eight cheerleaders."

Lowering their voices, Jennifer and Miss Green continued to discuss the problem.

"Hey—what's going on?"

Startled by the intrusion, both the captain and the advisor whirled around to see Kimmy standing in the doorway, hands on hips, her cheeks pink, breathing heavily.

"Can you ask Ronnie to come in?" Jennifer asked Kimmy. "We can only make room for one more girl, so Ronnie will have to—"

"Huh? You're putting those sisters on the squad?" Kimmy demanded, her voice rising several octaves.

"Of course," Jennifer replied. "You saw how good they were. They're awesome!"

21

"But I thought—" Kimmy stopped, letting the news sink in.

"We're very lucky they moved to Shadyside," Miss Green added with unusual enthusiasm.

"And that means—Ronnie's out?" Kimmy asked, her voice revealing her outrage. "She's off the squad? Just like that?"

"Kimmy—" Jennifer started.

But Miss Green took over, climbing to her feet as if prepared to fight. "Ronnie is only a freshman," she said firmly. "She'll be an alternate. She'll practice with the squad. And she'll go on if one of you gets sick or something."

"Oh, she'll *love* that," Kimmy said bitterly. "I really don't think it's fair. I mean—"

"Kimmy—you *saw* how good Bobbi and Corky are!" Jennifer cried. "We *need* them. We really do."

Kimmy started to reply, thought better of it, and uttered a sigh of exasperation. Glaring at Jennifer, she turned away from the office and called to Ronnie.

"You wanted to see me?" Ronnie hesitated in the doorway, nervously pushing back her curly red hair with both hands. She had small brown eyes, a tiny round stub of a nose, and a face full of freckles.

She almost collapsed when Miss Green told her of her demotion. Angry tears formed in the corners of her eyes, which she quickly wiped away with the backs of her hands.

"We really don't have a choice," Jennifer said softly.

"Yes, you do," Ronnie snapped back, her dark eyes flashing.

22

"We have to think of what's best for the squad," Miss Green said, twirling a pen nervously between her fingers. "You'll have plenty of opportunity—"

"Yeah. Sure," Ronnie interrupted, and fled toward the locker room.

"She feels bad," Jennifer said, staring through the glass as the other girls stopped their practice to watch Ronnie run off.

"She'll get over it," Miss Green said flatly.

"I'll never forgive them!" Ronnie cried. "Never!"

Kimmy and Debra huddled around the freshman, trying to ignore the steamy, junglelike air of the locker room. The other girls had showered and left. These three remained, talking, commiserating with one another, trying to decide what, if anything, they could do.

"Those sisters had no right to try out," Kimmy agreed heatedly, putting a comforting hand on Ronnie's shoulder.

"Not them," Ronnie insisted angrily. "Jennifer and Miss Green. It was *their* idea to kick me off."

"We should all get together," Debra said heatedly. "You know. Sign a petition or something. I'm sure Megan and Heather would sign it too." She sat down on the bench and began to pull off her sneakers.

Kimmy removed a white towel from her locker and mopped her forehead with it. "Wow, do I need a shower! Yeah, maybe you're right, Deb. If the whole squad protests, if we all stand together, I'll bet we could get them to change their minds."

Ronnie groaned and rolled her eyes. "What dream world do you live in?" she muttered. "The Corcoran sisters were all-state, remember? Did you see the look on Miss Green's face when they did that shoulder stand and all those double cartwheels?"

"She was practically drooling," Debra said, shaking her head. "She could probably see the championship trophy on her shelf."

"But what's Jennifer's problem?" Kimmy demanded, pulling her heavy sweater over her head.

"She's *your* friend," Ronnie said bitterly.

"I can't *believe* her," Debra added. "Maybe being captain has gone to her head or something. She thinks she's such a big deal."

"My parents are going to be very upset," Ronnie said with renewed sadness. "They were more excited about my making the squad than I was. And now—"

Kimmy and Debra continued trying to comfort Ronnie as they undressed, tossing their clothes onto the benches. They carried their towels over the concrete floor to the shower room.

"I don't *want* to be an alternate," Ronnie complained, her voice breaking with emotion. "That's just stupid. I'd rather—"

"If only the Corcorans would just go back where they came from," Debra said. "With their long blond hair and their big eyes and phony smiles." She put a finger down her throat and pretended to puke. "Yuck."

"They're not that bad," Ronnie muttered. "It's Jennifer. She had no right—"

Kimmy stepped under the chrome shower head. She turned the knobs on the wall with both hands.

The water burst out in a loud rush.

Kimmy froze openmouthed for a brief second.

Then she started to scream.

Chapter 4

A Tragic Accident

Kimmy staggered back until she hit the tile wall.

Panting loudly, she pointed to the water rushing in a broad stream from the shower head.

"Kimmy—are you okay?" Debra cried in alarm. "What *is* it?"

"The water—it's scalding hot!" Kimmy told her.

The three girls turned off the taps and hurried out, clutching their towels.

"Ow, that *burned!*" Kimmy declared, starting to breathe normally.

"Should we get the nurse? Are you all right?" Debra asked, staring at Kimmy's chest and neck, which were scarlet.

"I think I'll be okay," Kimmy said, relieved, covering herself with the towel. "It was just such a shock."

"We'll have to remember to tell Simmons," Debra said. And then she added sarcastically, "Maybe he'll get around to fixing it in a year or two."

Simmons was one of the Shadyside High custodians. He also drove a school bus. A laid-back young man with a blond ponytail and Walkman headphones that seemed to be permanently glued to his ears, he wasn't terribly reliable in either job.

"Hey—did you drop this?" Ronnie asked. She bent down and picked something shiny off the floor.

"Oh. Thanks." Kimmy reached out for it. It was her silver megaphone pendant. Her parents had given it to her for her sixteenth birthday. She struggled to put it back around her neck, which was still red from the scalding shower. "The clasp is loose," she said, frowning. "I really have to get it fixed. Don't want to lose it."

The three friends hurriedly got dressed in silence.

Hoisting her backpack onto her shoulder, Ronnie sighed and headed for the door, her sneakers thudding heavily on the concrete.

"You feeling any better?" Kimmy called after her.

"No" was the sullen reply.

"This is so exciting!" Bobbi declared.

It was a Friday evening, two weeks later, and the cheerleaders were boarding the small yellow and black school bus that would take them to the Tigers' first away game.

Corky followed her sister onto the bus. She said hi to Simmons, who was slouched in the driver's seat, fiddling with his ponytail. He grunted in reply.

27

Raindrops dotted the windshield. A light rain had started to fall. The sky was a gloomy charcoal color, but not gloomy enough to darken the sisters' moods.

They had been working hard for that night, practicing the new routines after school and at home, learning the cheers, working up a few new wrinkles of their own.

"Go, Tigers!" Bobbi yelled, tumbling into a seat near the back.

"Go *who??*" Megan yelled.

The bus quickly filled with loud, excited voices, happy laughter. Simmons leaned forward and pulled the handle to close the door.

"Hey—where's Miss Green?" Debra called.

Jennifer turned around in the front seat. "She's driving in her own car tonight. She had to take some friends."

Kimmy sat in the window seat next to Debra. She rubbed her hand over the glass, trying to clear the thin film of steam away so she could see out.

"Hey, Simmons—how about some air-conditioning?" one of the girls yelled. "We're melting back here!"

Simmons, obviously lost in his own thoughts, ignored the request, as usual. He started the bus up and clicked on the headlights.

Corky, seated in the aisle beside her sister, turned to stare out their window as the bus backed out of its parking space and headed out of the student parking lot. Rivulets of rainwater ran down the glass, distorting her view.

The rain picked up, drumming noisily on the roof

of the bus. A gust of wind blew water through the window, which was open an inch or two at the top. Bobbi raised herself up and, with great effort, pushed the window shut.

"Now we'll suffocate," Corky complained.

"Take your pick—suffocate or drown," Bobbi told her.

"Tough choice," Corky replied.

"Go, Tigers!" someone yelled.

Someone started a cheer, and everyone joined in.

> *"Tigers are yellow,*
> *Tigers are black.*
> *Push 'em back, push 'em back,*
> *Push 'em waaaaay back!"*

Bobbi smiled at her sister. She settled back in her seat, happy and excited.

The past two weeks had been difficult. The other girls were aloof at first, even resentful. But Bobbi was confident that she and Corky had won most of them over. Kimmy and Debra were still cold to them, still acted as if they were unwanted intruders. But she felt sure that she and Corky would eventually win those two over too.

As the bus rattled down Park Drive away from the school, the rain pounded harder. The trees and shrubs exploded in a white flash of lightning. The thunder seemed to crack right above them.

Heather and Megan began chanting, "Rain, rain, go away."

Jennifer turned in her seat to face the rest of the

29

cheerleaders. "It's not going to last," she announced. "It's just a flash storm. They said on the radio it's going to pass quickly."

Another loud thunderclap made two girls scream.

Everyone else laughed.

The big wipers scraped noisily, rhythmically, across the windshield, which was covered with a curtain of white steam. Simmons didn't seem to mind—or notice—the poor visibility.

Holding on to the seat-back, Jennifer stood up. "I have a few announcements to make," she called out, shouting to be heard over the driving rain.

Kimmy and Debra were giggling loudly about something. Jennifer waited for them to get quiet. "First of all, unless it's still drizzling, we'll do the fire baton routine at halftime as planned," Jennifer said, cupping her hands like a megaphone.

Simmons made a sharp turn onto Canyon Road, causing Jennifer to topple back into her seat. She pushed herself back up, flashing the driver an annoyed look, which, of course, he didn't see.

"If the storm doesn't blow over—" Jennifer continued.

"Oh no!" Corky cried. "The fire batons!"

All eyes turned to the back of the bus.

A flash of lightning seemed to outline Corky and her sister.

"We have to turn around!" Corky declared, shouting over the clap of thunder.

"What?" Jennifer called, her face filled with confusion.

"We have to stop at my house," Corky explained.

"The fire batons. Bobbi and I brought them home to practice. We forgot them. Can we turn around?"

Several girls groaned, Kimmy the loudest of all.

"It's only a small detour," Bobbi said, coming to her sister's defense.

"No problem," Jennifer said, her expression troubled. Standing in the aisle beside Simmons, she tapped him hard on the shoulder.

No reaction.

So she tugged his ponytail. "We have to make a stop on Fear Street," Jennifer told him.

"Huh?"

"Fear Street," Jennifer repeated impatiently. "Just turn here."

Simmons turned the wheel, and the bus skidded into a turn over the wet pavement. Holding on to the seat-back, Jennifer turned back to Corky and Bobbi. "Direct us when we get to Fear Street, okay?"

The two sisters agreed, apologizing again for the detour.

"Oooh, Fear Street," someone said, uttering a spooky howl. Some other girls laughed.

Kimmy made some kind of wisecrack to Debra, and the two girls giggled together.

The rain fell in heavy sheets, driven by unpredictable, powerful wind gusts. For some reason Simmons sped up. In front of him the big wipers swam mechanically across the steamy windshield.

Jennifer resumed her position in the aisle beside him. "I have just a few more announcements to make," she shouted.

Staring out the window at the storm, Bobbi saw the

passing houses and trees grow darker, as if a heavy shadow had lowered itself over them, over the whole world. Trees bent in the strong wind. The rain suddenly shifted and blew against the window, startling Bobbi and blocking her view.

Up at the front, Jennifer continued with her announcements. Bobbi couldn't hear her over the pounding rain, the thunder, the angry rush of wind.

Suddenly Simmons reached out and pulled the lever to open the door. The sound of the rain grew louder. Cold, wet air cut through the bus.

"Why did he open the door?" Corky asked her sister.

"I guess to see better," Bobbi replied thoughtfully. "The windshield is totally steamed."

"Are we near home?"

The bus sped up. Simmons had his head turned to the open door, his eyes on the cross street, which passed by in a gray blur.

Bobbi stared hard out the rain-blotted window, trying to read a street sign.

Suddenly she realized that something was wrong.

The bus—it began to skid.

There was no time to scream or cry out a warning.

One second they were moving along through the rain. The next second they were sliding, sliding out of control toward the curb.

"Whoa!" Simmons shrieked over the squeal of tires. "The brakes—!"

The tire squeals grew to a roar in Bobbi's ears. She covered them with both hands. She tried to scream, but the sound caught in her throat.

The impact was fast and hard.

What had they hit? A tree? A rock? The curb?

The bus seemed to bounce, to fly up off the road, to bounce again.

Staring in horror and surprise at the front, Bobbi saw Jennifer's eyes open wide. And then as the bus jolted and spun, she watched as Jennifer flew out the open door.

Jennifer's startled scream was drowned out by the squeal of the skidding tires.

By the crunch of metal.

By the shatter of glass.

Chapter 5

Death of a Cheerleader

It all took a second. Maybe less.

Bobbi blinked—and it was over.

The screams swirled around her, surrounding her.

She wasn't sure whether she was hearing the squeal of the tires or the cries of the cheerleaders.

And then the world tilted on its side.

With a silent, choked gasp, Bobbi toppled onto Corky. And the two of them, arms flailing helplessly, fell sideways toward the far window.

Which was now the floor.

No time to scream.

It took only a microsecond. Or so it seemed.

The window glass beneath them cracked all the way down the pane like a jagged bolt of lightning.

And still the bus bumped and slid, metal grating against pavement, invading their ears.

Bobbi felt another hard bump. A stab of pain jolted her entire body, made her shake and bounce.

And then all movement stopped. Such an abrupt stop. Such a shattering stop.

I'm okay, Bobbi realized. Her first clear thought.

She was on top of her sister, their arms and legs tangled.

Corky is okay too.

Corky stared up at her openmouthed, her green eyes wide with fear.

All sideways.

She heard muffled cries. Whimpers, like frightened puppies.

"Oh, man." A loud groan from the front of the bus. From Simmons.

Bobbi pulled herself up. Simmons was trying to stand. But everything was tilted. Everything was wrong.

"Are you okay?" Corky asked in a tiny voice.

"Yeah. I think so," Bobbi replied uncertainly.

"Then get *off* me!" Corky cried.

She sounded so angry, it made Bobbi laugh.

Hysterical laughter, she realized, and forced herself to stop.

Got to keep control. Control. Control.

Bobbi looked up to find a row of windows above her head.

"Oh," she said out loud. She finally realized what had happened. The bus was on its side.

It had rammed into a tree or something, bounced off and toppled onto its side, then skidded to a stop.

"How do we get out?" She heard Kimmy call even though she couldn't see her.

In the darkness she saw a tangle of arms and legs.

She heard a girl crying. She heard groans and whispers.

"The emergency door. In back!" someone shouted.

Bobbi reached for the emergency door, and tried pushing it open. It was stuck.

"The windows are faster!" someone else cried.

Kimmy stood up, raised both arms high, struggled to slide one of the windows open. Bobbi, balancing uneasily, tried to do the same.

"Can't you get *off* me?" Corky asked impatiently.

"I'm *trying*, okay?" Bobbi replied, not recognizing her own tight, shrill voice.

The window slid open.

Raindrops hit Bobbi's upturned face. Cold. Fresh. So clean.

"Is anyone hurt?" Simmons was calling, a tall shadow in the front. "Is anyone hurt? Who's crying?"

Bobbi raised herself up, grabbed hold of the window frame.

"Is anyone hurt?"

The rain was just a drizzle now. The rumble of thunder was low and far in the distance.

Bobbi pulled herself halfway out of the bus.

The whole world was shimmering, glistening, wet. Fresh and clean.

The bus tires were still spinning.

Where are we? Bobbi wondered. It all looked so familiar and unfamiliar at the same time.

Another face appeared. Debra was emerging from a window closer to the front. "Are you okay?" she called, squinting at Bobbi as if she were far away.

"I think so," Bobbi replied. "You?"

"Yeah. My wrist—I think it's sprained. That's all."

They pulled themselves out, smiled at each other, buoyed by the fresh air, the cool wetness, of being alive. Then standing on the overturned side that was now the roof, they leaned down into the windows to help other girls escape.

Time seemed to stand still.

Corky joined her sister, slid to the ground, stretched and yawned as if emerging from a long sleep.

The bus headlights, one on top of the other, cut through the air, casting twin spotlights on the jagged tombstones poking up through tall weeds.

Tombstones? Weeds?

Bobbi lowered herself to the ground, her sneakers sinking into the wet grass. Gripping Corky's ice-cold hand, she turned back toward the street.

Behind them, a tilted street sign read: FEAR ST.

"Oh." She let go of Corky's hand. "Look."

The bus had careened off the road and slid over the grass of the Fear Street cemetery. A thick yellow mist, catching the light from the headlights, lingered between the old gravestones, which rose up like arms and legs from the twisting, bending weeds.

"We're . . . in the cemetery," Corky said, her voice a whisper, her expression stunned. "How?"

"We're only a block from home," Bobbi said.

"Is everybody out?" Simmons called. He came toward them, taking long strides, his jeans stained at the knees, a bandanna wrapped tightly around a bleeding cut on his arm. "You okay?" he asked the two sisters.

"Yeah," Bobbi told him.

"Everyone got out," Simmons said. "No one's hurt too bad."

Then Bobbi and Corky cried out at the same time: "Jennifer!"

Where was Jennifer?

In the horror of the crash, in the noise and tilting darkness of it, they had forgotten about her.

Jennifer. Bobbi saw her again. Saw her arms jerk up as she flew out the open bus door—almost as if being pulled out.

"Jennifer?" Corky began calling, cupping her hands over her mouth. "Has anyone seen Jennifer?"

"Jennifer. Jennifer."

The word buzzed through the group of dazed, frightened girls as they huddled together, squinting against the bright headlights, trying to turn things right side up in their minds.

Trying to make sense of everything.

Trying to convince themselves that they were okay. That everything was going to be fine.

"Jennifer. Jennifer."

And then Corky saw her.

From behind.

Saw her body sprawled facedown, her head resting on the earth in front of an old tombstone, her arms stretched above her head as if she were hugging the stone.

"Jennifer!" Bobbi shouted.

A sudden gust of wind made Jennifer's skirt ruffle. But Jennifer didn't look up, didn't raise her head.

Corky and Bobbi reached her before the others. Bobbi grabbed her shoulders to roll her onto her back.

"Don't move her!" someone yelled.

"Don't touch her! It isn't safe!"

Bobbi looked up to see Simmons standing beside her, staring down at Jennifer sprawled so awkwardly across the old grave site.

"Let's carefully roll her over and get her face out of the mud," he said quietly.

They tugged her gently by the shoulders.

As they turned Jennifer over, the words etched on the old grave marker came into Bobbi's view: SARAH FEAR. The dates beneath the name had been worn away nearly beyond recognition: 1875–1899.

They laid Jennifer gently onto her back.

"Call an ambulance!" Heather was screaming. "Somebody—call for help!"

Bobbi leaned over Jennifer's unmoving form. "It's too late," she said, choking out the words. "She's dead."

Chapter 6

"It's Your Fault!"

"**N**o!"

Corky's anguished cry cut through the air. She dropped to the wet ground beside Jennifer and grabbed her pale, limp hand.

"No!"

At first Bobbi thought the low wail she was hearing came from her sister. But as the sound grew louder, cutting through the crackle and whisper of the wind bending the ancient trees of the cemetery, Bobbi realized it was the siren of an ambulance.

Someone in one of the houses across the street must have seen the accident and called for help.

A few seconds later three ambulances and a police cruiser pulled onto the wet grass, their flashing red lights washing over everyone, making everything seem too bright, the colors all wrong, too frightening, too vivid to be real.

The white coats of the paramedics, scrambling through the wet weeds, flashed red and gray, red and gray. The light caught their hard expressions like those in artificial-light snapshots, freezing them in Bobbi's mind. She knew she'd always remember every somber face, every flash of light, every second of this dark, wet nightmare.

Behind the tilted tombstone, Ronnie stood crying, sobbing loudly, her mouth open wide, her eyes round. Kimmy and Debra huddled around her, trying to comfort her, their faces distorted by the flickers of red light too.

The rain had stopped now, leaving the air heavy and cold.

On the ground in front of the tombstone, several paramedics worked over Jennifer, speaking softly among themselves, softly but urgently.

Gentle hands pulled Bobbi and her sister back. Two young police officers were questioning Simmons, who was shrugging and gesturing to the overturned bus. He appeared very frightened and upset.

Radios crackled from the ambulances and the police car. A paramedic leaning over Jennifer spoke rapidly into a cellular telephone. The wind blew a shower of ice-cold rainwater down from the trees.

Bobbi took a reluctant step closer.

Was Jennifer alive? Were they bringing her around? She had to see.

The white coats had formed a protective circle around Jennifer. Bobbi tried to make sense out of the buzz of low voices. She made her way to just outside the circle, her sneakers sinking into soft earth.

One of the paramedics stood up. In the blink of red

light, Bobbi saw his eyes close, his teeth clench. "She's gone," he said.

Another white-coated young man climbed to his feet, shaking his head.

"Gone."

Radios crackled. Ronnie's sobs cut through the air.

"No!" Bobbi screamed.

Without realizing it, without even realizing she was moving, Bobbi pushed past the grim-faced paramedics. She knelt at Jennifer's side, stared down at her pretty, expressionless face.

And Jennifer opened her eyes.

"Hey!" Bobbi cried. "Whoa!"

Jennifer blinked. And stared up at Bobbi.

"Hey—" Bobbi called. "Hey—"

Jennifer blinked again. Her lips trembled. Her dark eyes moved from side to side.

"Hey—she's alive!" Bobbi called. "Hey—"

Corky was holding on to Bobbi's shoulders, leaning over her, staring down at Jennifer.

Jennifer smiled up at them both.

"Hey—"

Cheers and cries. Urgent voices. The crackling of the radios. A low voice speaking rapidly into a cellular phone.

The sounds were drowned out by a rush of wind. It started to rain again.

Bobbi stared at the flashing colors, the darting yellow cones of light from the flashlights, the pale white beams of headlights. The lights all melted into one and grew brighter and brighter until she had to close her eyes.

Jennifer was alive. Okay. She was going to be okay.

Her eyes still shut tightly, Bobbi said a silent prayer.

When she opened her eyes, Jennifer's gurney was being gently slid into an ambulance. Two more squad cars had pulled up. Several officers stood outlined in headlights, inspecting the overturned bus, shaking their heads.

"Lucky no one was killed."

The words floated through the air and repeated in Bobbi's mind.

The rain came down harder, swirled by the wind.

The ambulance siren started with a cough. Then the shrill wail corkscrewed through the rustling trees. The ambulance roared away.

"How will we get home?" Ronnie was asking, still flanked by Kimmy and Debra.

"What about the game?" Heather asked.

"We have to get *home!*" Ronnie insisted.

"Will Jennifer be okay?"

"Has anyone called our parents?"

"Someone should call Miss Green."

"She's probably at the game."

"They won't play in this rain."

Let it rain, Bobbi thought, raising her face to it. Let the rain wash everything away. Everything.

She turned, startled to see Kimmy standing beside her, a cold, grim expression on her face, her eyes locked on Bobbi's.

"Kimmy—?" Bobbi started.

"This is all your fault," Kimmy said, speaking through clenched teeth. Her hands were balled into tight fists at her sides. The rain had matted her black hair against her forehead.

"Huh?"

"All your fault," Kimmy repeated, continuing to glare at Bobbi. "If you hadn't made us turn onto Fear Street—"

"Now, *wait* a minute!" Bobbi cried. "That isn't fair!"

She realized the other cheerleaders were all staring at her, their faces grim and unhappy, lit by the flashes of red light.

"Kimmy, that's not fair," Corky cried, rushing forward to join her sister.

Kimmy walked quickly back to Ronnie and Debra.

"That's not fair!" Corky repeated.

The rain fell harder, making it difficult to see. The ambulance carrying Jennifer was far in the distance now, its siren a lingering cry that refused to fade away.

PART TWO

The Fall

Chapter 7

The New Captain

The cheers thundered down from the bleachers as the cheerleaders ran out onto the floor. As the seven girls bounded across the gym, the noise rose and echoed until it felt as if the roof might be blown off.

Kimmy led the girls onto the floor, and they immediately went into what they called their clap-clap routine. The girls clapped out a rhythm—and everyone in the bleachers repeated it as loudly as possible.

As she clapped, Kimmy stared up at the colorful blur of kids filling the bleachers, spilling out onto the gym floor, standing along the walls. The entire school was at the pep rally.

The hand clapping gave way to foot stomping. The bleachers quaked and trembled. The rhythm picked up. Faster. Louder.

What a thrill! Kimmy thought, an excited grin

47

spread across her face. What a thrill to perform for the entire school! What a *sound!* Like an earthquake or the stampede of a thousand elephants!

She knew she looked great in her new uniform. They all did. The maroon and white was so sharp, the skirt so crisp, and the sweater so bright. Their old uniforms had been ruined that night in the rain.

But here it was, two weeks later, and everything was fresh and new again. And everyone was cheering. Cheering their lungs out.

Well . . . almost everyone.

"Give me a T!"

"T!"

"Give me an I!"

"I!"

"Give me a G!"

"G!"

What a sound! Kimmy thought, her grin growing even wider as her shiny black hair bounced around her face every time she jumped.

They finished the cheer in a wavelike ripple, the girls going down in splits one after the other. Kimmy glanced down the row of cheerleaders, all so happy, so fresh and excited, as if that terrible night had never happened.

There was Ronnie down at the end, radiant, shouting her heart out. Her curly red hair, caught in the bright lights, seemed to glow on its own. How happy she'd been to be back on the squad.

And Debra, normally so cool, so withdrawn, was cheering at the top of her lungs.

Only cheerleaders, Kimmy thought, know what this

is like. A lot of people put us down. They think we're wasting our time. Or we're out-of-date or something. But that's because they don't know this special excitement, the special thrill of getting a huge crowd to forget itself and go wild.

The cheer ended to raucous shouts and applause.

Kimmy peered down the line of girls to see Corky and Bobbi do their special double cartwheel.

Ugh, she thought bitterly. What showoffs. They really make me sick. With their blond hair and sweet, innocent faces. Always prancing around together, trying to make the rest of us look second rate. I could throw up. I really could.

The echoing drums of the marching band brought Kimmy out of her dark thoughts.

No, she decided. I'm not going to allow those two to ruin this day. I'm not going to give them another thought.

Everyone stood and clapped along as the band played the Shadyside High marching song.

I want only good memories of this pep rally, Kimmy thought, clapping as hard as she could. After all, the rally is in honor of *us,* in honor of how brave we were, in honor of how we survived that terrible night.

The band ended its number to wild applause. Corky and Bobbi did their cartwheel again, and Kimmy forced herself not to react.

The girls all turned to her to begin the next cheer routine.

"Let's go, let's go, let's go, let's go. . . ."

Kimmy's eye caught Miss Green leaning against the

wall of her office and clapping along with them, a big smile on her usually dour face.

In a few minutes Miss Green will name me as the new captain, Kimmy thought. The thought sent a shiver of excitement down her back.

It's something I've wanted for so long. I've worked so hard for it, so hard.

I'm not knockout beautiful like the other girls. I'm not tall and well built. I don't have straight blond hair like the Corcorans or look like a movie star like . . . Jennifer.

But I'm going to be captain. I'm finally going to be captain.

She wished her parents could have been there to see it, to see the pep rally, to see their daughter, to see how exciting it all was. She had begged them to come. But, as usual, they claimed they couldn't get away from their jobs.

Just an excuse, Kimmy thought bitterly.

Then forced those thoughts out of her mind. Nothing was going to spoil her day. Nothing.

Whoa!

The routine ended. The band started up immediately. Kimmy turned toward the far side of the gym, and the other girls followed her lead.

As the band finished its number, a deafening cheer went up as Jennifer wheeled herself out onto the floor. She was wearing a new uniform too, Kimmy saw. In her hand was a maroon and white pennant with her name embroidered on it, the pennant they had given her in the hospital.

She waved it from her seat as she vigorously

wheeled herself across the gym. The applause grew and grew until Kimmy felt like covering her ears.

Jennifer has been so brave during all this, Kimmy thought, staring at her in her wheelchair now lined up with the other cheerleaders.

So brave and cheerful, even though she might never walk again.

Even though her life was ruined.

Kimmy wondered if *she* would have been so brave, so smiling, so . . . accepting.

Of course, Jennifer had nearly died that night, Kimmy remembered. Everyone had thought she *was* dead. So in a way she was lucky, lucky just to be alive.

But how could anyone consider being crippled, perhaps for life, lucky?

Kimmy realized that the gym had grown silent. Jennifer had wheeled herself to a microphone and begun a short speech.

"I'm not good at making speeches," she was saying, her voice so weak and unsteady. "I'd much rather be cheering than talking!"

Nervous laughter rolled down from the bleachers. One of the drummers in the band hit a rim shot.

"I just want to say thank you to everyone at Shadyside High," Jennifer continued, her voice breaking with sudden emotion. "You've all been so good to me . . . all my friends . . . everyone . . . with all the cards and presents and stuff. . . ." She waved the pennant. "And I just want to tell you all that . . . I feel *great!* Go, Tigers!"

She pushed back from the microphone, waving her pennant, as the entire school erupted in applause. The band played the marching song again. Maroon and white streamers came flying down from the bleachers.

Kimmy wiped away the tears that were rolling down her cheeks. She could feel herself begin to lose control, feel the loud, choking sobs try to force their way up.

But she cut them off.

This wasn't a sad day. It was a happy day.

Everyone was smiling and cheering.

This was a celebration. A celebration that they were all alive.

So why did Jennifer's smile make Kimmy feel like bawling?

She turned away from Jennifer. It was the only way to keep the sobs down, to keep herself in control.

I'm just excited, she thought. Overexcited, I guess.

She took a deep breath and held it.

Miss Green was approaching them, taking long strides across the gleaming wood gym floor, an intent expression on her face. She wore a maroon and white Shadyside sweatshirt over gray sweat pants. As she neared the microphone, her face flushed, she clasped her hands together behind her back.

Miss Green hated public speaking. She seldom spoke at assemblies or pep rallies, and when she did, she always rocked back and forth on her feet and her voice quavered, and everyone could tell she was really nervous.

She smiled at Jennifer, stopped, and made a short bow to her. Then, her face nearly scarlet, she stepped close to the microphone.

"I have an announcement to make!" she shouted, her voice echoing off the four walls. It took a while for the crowd to quiet down. She stood silently, waiting until they did. Kimmy could see a muscle twitch in her jaw from nervousness.

Poor woman, she thought sympathetically.

Kimmy felt the excitement begin to tighten her own muscles. She realized she was smiling with trembling lips. She hoped no one could see them shaking.

"This is a day of celebration," Miss Green began. "We are celebrating the great spirit of these Shadyside cheerleaders. And we are celebrating the spirit shown in particular by Jennifer Daly."

The gym grew absolutely silent. So silent, Kimmy could hear a car horn honking outside in the parking lot.

"We are all celebrating today because Jennifer is back with us," Miss Green continued, rocking on the heels of her white high-tops. "Her courage, her strength, her indomitable spirit, are an example for us all."

Applause.

"Now it's time for me to announce a new captain," Miss Green said, glancing at Jennifer, who flashed her an encouraging smile.

Kimmy took a deep breath. Her heart was thudding so hard, she thought she might pass out.

She gave Jennifer a big smile, but Jennifer had turned to stare up into the bleachers.

"I have spent many hours thinking about this selection," Miss Green continued. "And I know that the young lady I have chosen will lead the Tiger cheerleaders with the same courage and spirit that Jennifer Daly has shown."

Yes! Yes! Thank you! Kimmy thought, about to burst.

She took another deep breath and let it out slowly.

Miss Green cleared her throat and then, speaking loudly and enthusiastically, announced the name of the new cheerleader captain.

"No!" Kimmy shrieked out loud. "Please—no!"

Chapter 8

Kimmy Quits

Kimmy's cries of protest were drowned out by the applause that rang down from the bleachers. Several of the other cheerleaders, including Ronnie and Debra, had turned to Kimmy to watch her mouth drop open and her expression turn to shock and dismay.

Bobbi Corcoran?

How could Bobbi Corcoran be named cheerleader captain?

Unfair, Kimmy thought, feeling her surprise turn to rage. *Impossible!*

After all, Kimmy had been named assistant captain last spring. She had been on the squad for two years. She had worked so hard. So hard.

So how could she be passed over for a flashy newcomer?

Bobbi had been on the squad for only a few weeks. She didn't know the school. She didn't know any of the routines.

So how could Miss Green and Jennifer have chosen her?

Kimmy stood with her shoulders slumped forward, allowing her unhappiness, her anger, to show on her face. She was miserable and upset, and she didn't care who knew it.

As the applause died down and Miss Green continued talking, Kimmy glanced down the line of cheerleaders. There was Corky hugging her sister joyfully. Heather and Megan had rushed over to congratulate Bobbi. And Bobbi had the widest smile on her face, her eyes brimming with happy tears.

Yuck, Kimmy thought bitterly.

I know why she was named captain. Because she's so pretty, and I'm not. She's so blond and skinny and disgustingly all-American.

Okay. So I'm not skinny, and I don't have long blond hair and look like a *Seventeen* model. But how could Jennifer and Miss Green *do* this to me? I'm a better cheerleader than Bobbi Corcoran ever will be!

I deserve to be captain. Everyone knows I deserve to be captain.

Kimmy realized then that her entire body was trembling. Staring up into the bleachers, she felt her anger turn to embarrassment.

Everyone is staring at me, she decided. Everyone in the entire school. They're all staring at me. They know I deserve to be captain. They know I've been cheated.

She turned and saw Debra and Ronnie studying her, their faces locked in sympathy, their eyes on Kimmy's face, trying to determine how Kimmy was taking the awful news.

Everyone is watching me, Kimmy thought, forcing back the loud sobs that pushed at her throat. Everyone is feeling sorry for me.

I've never been so embarrassed.

This is the worst day of my life.

I'll never forgive Bobbi. Never.

And I'll never forgive Miss Green either.

I just want to disappear. I just want to *die*.

And as bitter thoughts continued to spin through Kimmy's mind, Miss Green finished her remarks and stepped back from the microphone with a relieved sigh. There was a scattering of applause.

Kimmy saw Jennifer smiling, always smiling that brave smile of hers, wheeling herself to the side of the gym.

And then Bobbi—*Bobbi!*—led the girls into a circle to begin their final routine.

No! Kimmy decided.

No way.

I can't do this. I'm too embarrassed. Too humiliated. I won't do it. I *won't!*

I quit, she decided.

I quit the cheerleaders.

She had joined the circle, followed the others automatically like some kind of a sheep. But now, as they raised their arms high in the air to begin their routine, Kimmy uttered a cry of disgust—and took off, running across the polished wood floor. Running, running as fast as she could, her eyes narrowed, nearly shut, her heart pounding in rhythm with each thud of her sneakers.

Were those gasps of surprise from the bleachers? Were those startled questions? A worried buzz of voices?

Kimmy didn't care. She was escaping. Escaping and never coming back.

As she reached the double doors to the corridor, running so hard she nearly collided with them, she turned and glanced back. The cheer had begun without her; Corky Corcoran had moved around to close up the circle.

I'll pay her back too, Kimmy decided.

Jennifer. Bobbi. Corky. All of them.

She was through the doors and running down the empty corridor when the first anguished sob finally burst from her throat.

Chapter 9

Bobbi and Chip

"Congratulations!"

Bobbi pulled open her locker door and turned to greet a girl she didn't know. "Thanks," she said, smiling.

"I'm Cari Taylor," the girl said, shifting the books she was carrying. She was a pretty, fragile-looking girl with blond hair, even lighter and finer than Bobbi's, and a warm, friendly smile. "I have science lab sixth period too. I've seen you there."

"Yeah. Right," Bobbi replied. "I've seen you too."

"I just wanted to say hi and congratulations," Cari said with a shrug. Then she added, "That accident must have been scary."

"Yeah," Bobbi said. "It was."

"Well, see you tomorrow."

"Right. See you."

The long corridor was emptying out as kids headed for home or after-school jobs. Bobbi could still hear the ringing applause in her ears, the cheers, the shouts, the pounding of the drums echoing off the walls.

Wow! I just feel so *great!* Bobbi thought, pulling some books and a binder from the top shelf of her locker. I feel as if I could *fly* home!

A few other kids, kids she'd seen around school but didn't really know, called out congratulations as they passed by. Maybe Shadyside High is an okay place, Bobbi thought happily.

During her first weeks in school, she had wondered if she'd ever get to like it. The kids all seemed so snobby. They all seemed to have known each other their whole lives. Bobbi wondered if she'd ever fit in or find friends of her own.

But that day had erased all of her worries. It was going to be a great school year, Bobbi decided. Great. Great. Great. Everything was great.

Still in her cheerleader uniform, she looked up and down the hall. Seeing that it was empty, she performed a high leap, landed, and did a cartwheel that nearly carried her into the wall.

Having gotten that out of her system, she collected her books, stuffed them into her backpack, and humming to herself, headed out the back door to the student parking lot.

Even the weather is great today, she thought, stopping to take a deep breath. The afternoon sky was still high and cloudless. The air felt warm and dry, more like summer than a day in autumn.

Near the fence, two girls sat on the hood of a car,

talking to a boy in a maroon and white letter jacket. Beside them, another car revved up noisily. Two boys were puzzling over a bike with a flat rear tire, scratching their heads and scowling.

Beyond the student parking lot, Shadyside Park stretched out, still green and vibrant. A broad, grassy field with an empty baseball diamond set in one corner led to thick woods.

I wish Mom and Dad were home, Bobbi thought. I can't wait to tell them the news.

I'm still in a state of shock, she told herself. It was such a surprise. I never *dreamed* that Miss Green would name me captain!

The other girls must have been shocked too, Bobbi realized. Especially Kimmy.

Kimmy.

She hadn't stopped to think about Kimmy. But now the thought descended on her like a heavy cloud, bringing her back to earth.

Had Kimmy come over to congratulate her? Bobbi struggled to remember. She had been surrounded by everyone all at once. But no. She didn't remember Kimmy being one of them.

I'd better call her or something, she thought.

Just then a hand touched her shoulder, startling her out of her thoughts.

"Hi."

She stared into a boy's face. He was handsome, with friendly dark brown eyes that crinkled at the corners, a shy smile, and lots of unbrushed brown hair that seemed to be tossed around on his head.

"Hi." She returned the greeting.

It was Chip Chasner, quarterback of the Tigers. She had seen him a lot during outdoor practices. He was friendly with the other cheerleaders, but he had never said a word to Bobbi.

He fell into step with her as she crossed the parking lot. He was broad shouldered and tall, especially in his shoulder pads and cleats.

"I just wanted to say, way to go," he said shyly, his dark eyes smiling at her.

"Thanks," she said, suddenly shy too. "I was really surprised. I mean, I didn't think they'd pick me. Since I'm new and all."

"We haven't really met. I'm Charles Chasner," he said. "But everyone calls me Chip."

"I know," Bobbi replied, feeling her face grow hot. "I think you're a really good player."

"Thanks." He beamed at her. Her compliment seemed to make him forget his shyness. "I've watched you too."

"Tough game Friday night," Bobbi said, watching the two boys dispiritedly walk the disabled bike away.

"Yeah. Winstead is always tough," Chip said, waving to a couple of girls who had just emerged from the building. "They'll probably cream us."

Bobbi laughed. "Wow, you've sure got confidence," she said sarcastically.

"No. Come on," he replied. "I'm pumped for the game. But you've got to be realistic. They went to the state finals last year."

"How'd you learn to throw the ball so far?" Bobbi asked, stopping at the edge of the parking lot, shifting her backpack on her shoulders. "Just practice a lot?"

"Yeah." He nodded. "My dad and I used to practice throwing in the backyard. We still do, when he has the time. He's working two jobs these days, so it's kind of tough."

"My parents both work all the time," Bobbi told him. "But I'm usually at cheerleading practice or studying, so I wouldn't see them much even if they were home."

"I guess my dad got me my first football when I was five," Chip said, leaning against the parking lot fence. The wind ruffled his thick, brown hair, his dark eyes studying Bobbi as he talked. "He loves football, but he never had a chance to play. Always had to work. So I guess he wanted to do his playing through me."

"That can be a lot of pressure," Bobbi said thoughtfully.

Chip's expression hardened. "I can handle it," he said softly.

"I just meant—" Bobbi started, surprised by his abrupt answer.

"Are you going out with anybody or anything?" Chip interrupted.

Caught off guard by the change of subject, Bobbi hesitated. "No," she finally managed to reply. "Are you?"

He shook his head. "No. Not anymore. Want to meet me after the Winstead game?" He stared at her intently. "We could go get a pizza. You know. Hang out with some other guys?"

"Great," Bobbi replied. "Sounds good."

"Well, okay. Excellent." He glanced up at the clock over the back door of the school. "I've got to practice," he said, pushing away from the fence. "After the game, wait for me outside the stadium locker room, okay?"

He didn't wait for her to reply. Instead, he slipped his helmet on and began jogging toward the practice field across from the baseball diamond, taking long, easy strides.

What an amazing day! Bobbi thought, watching him as he ran. So many good things happening at once!

She shook her head, somewhat dazed by it all. Her next thought was: I'll probably be hit by a truck on the way home.

The next evening, a warm, almost balmy Thursday night, Bobbi finished her dinner, then hurried to Jennifer's house to study. Since the accident, she and Jennifer had become close.

Unlike some of the other girls, who wanted to shut the accident out of their minds and forget it had ever happened, Bobbi had visited Jennifer in the hospital every day. Bobbi had been touched by her new friend's bravery and serenity. Soon she and Jennifer were talking easily, sharing their thoughts and feelings as if they had been longtime friends.

Bobbi parked her car on the street and made her way up the smooth asphalt drive. Jennifer lived in a sprawling, modern ranch house in North Hills, the wealthiest section of Shadyside.

What a contrast to Fear Street, Bobbi thought wistfully, her eyes taking in the manicured lawns, raked clean, and the well-cared-for houses.

The streetlights flickered on as Mrs. Daly opened the door to her. "Oh, hi, Bobbi," she said, looking tired and drawn in the pale porchlight. "Jennifer's waiting for you in the den."

Bobbi eagerly made her way across the carpeted living room with its low, sleek furniture of chrome and white leather and into the small den, closing the door behind her. "Did you talk to Kimmy?" she asked Jennifer, skipping any greeting.

Jennifer was seated in her wheelchair, between two red leather couches that faced each other. She was wearing navy blue sweats, the sweatshirt sleeves rolled up above her elbows. Her red-brown hair was tied behind her head in a single braid. She had a textbook in her lap.

"I talked to her," she replied, her face expressionless. Slowly a smile spread across her full lips. "She's coming back."

"Oh, good," Bobbi said, breathing a long sigh. She dropped her backpack on the checkered tile floor and plopped down in the red couch on Jennifer's right. "I can't believe I didn't even notice that she had run out."

"You were a little excited," Jennifer said dryly.

"But I should have known Kimmy would be upset," Bobbi insisted, rubbing her hand against the smooth leather of the couch arm. "But I didn't see her. I didn't see anything. It was all so . . ." She didn't finish her thought.

"Anyway, I talked to her," Jennifer said, wheeling herself closer until she was right in front of Bobbi. "She's not a happy camper, but I got her to come around." Her mouth fell into an unhappy pout. She avoided Bobbi's eyes. "Kimmy and I used to be so close. But not anymore."

"I'm really sorry," Bobbi said quickly. "If it's my fault, I—"

"No, it isn't," Jennifer interrupted. "You didn't do anything. Really."

"How did you get her to come back on the squad?" Bobbi asked.

"I told her we needed her. I said, 'What would happen if Bobbi fell and broke her leg?'"

"And what did *she* say?" Bobbi wondered.

"She asked if I would put that in writing!" Jennifer replied.

Both girls burst out laughing.

"Kimmy isn't your biggest fan," Jennifer said.

"Well, *duh,*" Bobbi replied, rolling her eyes, imitating her little brother, Sean. "Well, *duh*" was Sean's favorite expression.

"Well, I'm glad she's not quitting," Bobbi said.

"Really? Why?" Jennifer demanded, closing the textbook on her lap and tossing it onto the couch opposite Bobbi.

"Because . . . because it would make me feel really bad," Bobbi said with emotion.

Jennifer snickered. "Having her around might make you feel a lot worse, Bobbi. She won't talk to you. You know that. And she'll probably try to turn the other girls against you. I'm sure she's been on the phone night and day with those two pals of hers, Debra and Ronnie."

Bobbi sighed and pulled both hands back through

her hair. "You know, it's only a cheerleading squad. It's supposed to be fun."

"Tell that to Kimmy," Jennifer said softly. She shifted her weight in the wheelchair. "Ow."

"Are you okay?" Bobbi asked, leaning forward, preparing to jump up if her friend needed help of some kind.

"Yeah. Fine." Jennifer forced a smile. "Let's change the subject, okay?"

"Yeah. Okay." Bobbi settled back on the couch. "Do you know Charles Chasner?"

"Chip? Sure." Jennifer's smile broadened. "Chip is a real babe. I've had a crush on him since third grade. He's cuter now, though."

"He asked me out for tomorrow after the game," Bobbi confided.

Jennifer's eyes widened in surprise. "Huh? Chip?"

Bobbi nodded. "Yeah. He asked me out. Yesterday. After the pep rally."

"Really?"

Bobbi was startled to see Jennifer's eyes narrow and her features tighten. Jennifer glared at Bobbi. "You didn't say yes—*did* you?"

Chapter 10

Horror in the Hall

"Jen—what's wrong?" Bobbi asked.

Jennifer shook her head, then locked her eyes on Bobbi's. "Don't you know that Chip is Kimmy's boyfriend?"

"Huh?" Bobbi's mouth dropped open in shock. She suddenly could feel the blood pulsing at her temples.

"I mean, he *was* Kimmy's boyfriend," Jennifer said, gripping the sides of the wheelchair, "until a couple of weeks ago."

"A couple of weeks?"

"Yeah." Jennifer frowned. "Then he dumped her. Just like that. After more than two years."

"Oh, my gosh." Bobbi slumped down in the soft leather couch. She seemed to deflate. The shock of this news made her feel weak. "She'll think—"

"She'll think Chip dumped her for you," Jennifer finished the thought for her.

Bobbi moaned. "One more reason for Kimmy to hate my guts."

They stared at each other in silence for a while. Jennifer squeaked her wheelchair back and forth on the floor.

Finally Bobbi asked, "What should I do?"

Jennifer shrugged. "I don't know. He's *really* cute!"

"Girls, how about getting up a little energy?" Miss Green said. It was more of a complaint than a question, and she said the words with disgust.

Having blown her whistle and stepped onto the floor to interrupt the practice, she did an imitation of the way they looked to her, moving her arms and legs in weary slow motion, her eyes half-closed, her mouth drooping open.

The cheerleaders watched in sullen silence. Bobbi felt embarrassed. She was leading the practice, after all. It was *her* job to get the girls to show some spirit, not Miss Green's.

But Bobbi was finding it difficult to get some of the girls to listen to her, even though it was the last practice before the game that night.

Kimmy had done a good job of turning the girls against Bobbi. It hadn't been hard, Bobbi realized unhappily. The girls had all known Kimmy for years. Bobbi was a newcomer, an intruder.

Most of the cheerleaders hadn't wanted to allow the Corcorans on the squad in the first place. And now here was Bobbi, giving them instructions, leading them, or *trying* to lead them, *trying* to get them to cooperate.

"When you do 'Sssssssssteam Heat' like that," Miss

Green was scolding them, "it makes me think your boiler's broken."

It was supposed to be a joke, but it fell flat on the dispirited squad. No one even cracked a smile.

Standing beside Miss Green, Bobbi let her eyes wander down the row of girls. She stopped at Kimmy, who was glaring at her, her eyes narrowed. Kimmy's stare was so hard, so cold, it forced Bobbi to look away.

The gym doors opened, and Jennifer wheeled herself in. Smiling at Bobbi, she made her way silently along the far wall, her maroon and white pennant on her lap, her backpack attached to her wheelchair.

Bobbi wished Jennifer hadn't come. She felt embarrassed to have Jennifer show up while the girls were being lectured by Miss Green. Jennifer would see that Bobbi didn't have control, that the girls weren't with her.

She knew Jennifer would be sympathetic. She was Bobbi's best friend, after all. But it was still embarrassing.

Bobbi felt a hand on her shoulder. It was Corky, who gave her an encouraging smile and then quickly resumed her place.

Bobbi took a deep breath. "Okay, guys," she shouted, clapping her hands enthusiastically and moving in front of Miss Green, "let's try it again! Let's really get ssssteamed up!"

She saw Kimmy roll her eyes and sarcastically mutter something to Debra. Then the girls lined up and began the Steam Heat routine, this time with a little more enthusiasm than before.

It wasn't great. Ronnie was out of step for the entire last part of it, but Bobbi didn't think it was worth making them do it again.

As the routine ended with a cheer and a spread eagle, she turned to see Jennifer and Miss Green talking heatedly near the wall. Miss Green was leaning over the wheelchair, close to Jennifer's ear. Both of them were shaking their heads as they spoke.

Are they talking about me? Bobbi wondered, dread building in the pit of her stomach. Is Miss Green complaining about me, about how I haven't been able to win over the girls?

"Are we finished?"

Kimmy's shrill question made Bobbi turn back to the line of girls.

"Yeah. I guess," Bobbi said distractedly.

"Well, can we *go?*" Kimmy asked impatiently. "I mean, the game's in a few hours. We have to go home and have dinner and everything, *don't* we?"

Kimmy was making no attempt to hide her dislike of Bobbi. To her dismay, Bobbi saw that some of the other girls seemed to adopt Kimmy's attitude.

They all agree with her, Bobbi thought, her head suddenly pounding, her temples throbbing. They probably *all* think that Kimmy should be captain, not me.

And now even Jennifer and Miss Green are talking about me.

"We'll meet here in the gym at seven," Bobbi announced dispiritedly, avoiding their eyes by glancing up at the scoreboard clock. "Ronnie will be in charge of equipment."

Ronnie rolled her eyes and cast a glance at Kimmy.

"No fire batons tonight," Bobbi announced. "That routine needs a lot more work. We'll try it for homecoming next week."

The girls picked up their belongings and quickly made their way out of the gym. Bobbi stood in the middle of the floor, her shoulders slumped, feeling discouraged, watching the girls exit.

"I thought it went a lot better, that last time," Corky said, offering an encouraging smile.

"Liar," Bobbi muttered.

Corky shrugged. "No. Really."

"Thanks," Bobbi said dryly, watching Jennifer and Miss Green still talking animatedly.

"You coming straight home?" Corky bent to scratch one knee. Her hair was damp from perspiration.

At least one cheerleader is really trying, Bobbi thought miserably. "Go on without me," she told her sister. "I've got to get all my stuff."

Giving her a quick, playful salute, Corky obediently headed to the door. With a sigh, Bobbi turned and saw that Jennifer and Miss Green had disappeared into the advisor's office in the corner.

She pulled the whistle from around her neck and, swinging it by its cord, began walking slowly toward the door. Being cheerleader captain is supposed to be *fun,* she thought regretfully.

Well, she told herself, I'll find a way to win them over. Maybe even Kimmy. Once again she remembered Kimmy's cold stare, and shuddered.

She stepped into the hallway, which was empty and silent. Her sneakers squeaked along the hard floor. She turned a corner, climbed the stairs to the first floor, and headed to her locker to collect her books and jacket.

The long corridor stretched before her like a tunnel. The lights had been dimmed to save energy. Gray lockers lined both walls. The classrooms were dark and empty.

Bobbi coughed, the sound echoing through the long tunnel.

The loud crash behind her made her jump and cry out.

She spun around in time to see a locker door swing open, then slam shut.

"Oh!"

Another crash. In front of her.

She turned to see two lockers against the right wall swing open.

As she stared in disbelief, two more lockers pulled open. The doors seemed to hesitate, then slammed shut with deafening force.

Her mouth open in a silent cry, Bobbi gaped in astonishment.

Doors slammed, then swung open again.

Bang. Bang.

The sound echoed until it became a terrifying roar.

Bang. Bang. Both rows of locker doors swung open at once, as if pulled by invisible hands.

"No!" Bobbi cried.

This isn't happening. I'm *imagining* this!

Her heart pounding, she dropped the whistle and began to run. Past swinging, slamming locker doors. Through the echoing sounds, a barrage like gunfire.

"No! Stop!"

The wall of lockers on her left swung open in unison, then slammed shut with a deafening *crash*.

"No! Please!"

She held her hands over her ears and ran.

And then she heard the screams.

A girl, screaming in horror.

High-pitched, shrill screams of anguish, of pain.

Who's there? Bobbi wondered, running between the slamming lockers. Who *is* it?

The girl screamed again, the sound rising above the thunder of the lockers.

And again.

Bobbi's sneakers pounded against the floor. She ran blindly through the dark hallway, locker doors swinging open, then slamming shut on both sides of her.

Another scream of agony.

Bobbi reached the end of the corridor, turned the corner, and stared in surprise.

Chapter 11

Who Was Screaming?

No one there.

The front hall was deserted.

Silence.

"Hello?" Bobbi called.

No reply. No screams. The only sound now was that of her loud, gasping breaths.

"Hello? Anyone there?" she called out in a hoarse, choked voice.

Silence.

No one.

Confused and frightened, her hands pressed tightly to her burning cheeks, Bobbi turned back. And peered cautiously down the long, dim corridor.

The dark lockers along the walls were all shut tight.

Her ears rang from the crashing, banging sounds

they had made. But now they stood still and silent. She took a reluctant step, then another, expecting them to fly open again, to begin their frightening symphony.

Silence.

No lockers banging. No girl screaming in terror.

Her legs trembling, Bobbi made her way to her locker. She opened the combination lock with a shaking hand and pulled the door open.

She glanced down the hall. Still silent and empty.

The silence seemed to echo in her mind.

Am I cracking up?

Am I totally losing it?

She pulled out the things she needed, stuffed them into her backpack, locked the door, and ran.

At home, in the upstairs room they shared, Corky didn't believe her. "You're very tired," she said sympathetically from her desk, where she was trying to cram in a little homework before she had to leave for the game. "You've been under a lot of pressure."

"You don't believe me?" Bobbi shrieked, immediately angry at herself for not keeping her cool.

Corky stared at her sister thoughtfully. "Locker doors flying open?"

"I know it sounds crazy—" Bobbi started.

"The hall was dark, right?" Corky interrupted, tapping her pencil against her open textbook. "It was late. You were tired. Practice was rough. You're nervous about the game tonight."

Bobbi started to protest, then changed her mind. With a loud sigh, she tossed herself onto her bed. "I wouldn't believe me either," she muttered softly. "I wouldn't—"

She stopped and gasped in horror, staring across the room.

Corky followed her sister's frightened gaze.

Both girls watched in silent terror as the closet door swung open.

Chapter 12

Chip Is Buried

"It's—it's happening again," Bobbi uttered, her voice a choked whisper.

Corky raised her hands to her face, her eyes wide with fear, and stared openmouthed as the closet door continued to move.

And Sean stepped out, a triumphant grin spread across his face, his eyes sparkling with evil glee. "Hi," he said, giving them a nonchalant wave.

"Oh!" Bobbi jumped up, her hands balling into fists at her sides.

"You little creep!" Corky screamed. She grabbed Sean by the neck and pretended to choke him.

He collapsed to his knees in a fit of giggles.

"How long have you been in the closet?" Bobbi demanded, joining Corky in holding him down on the floor.

"It wasn't me. It was a ghost," he said.

Both girls began tickling him furiously.

"Ow! Ow! Ow!" he cried, squirming and laughing.

All three of them were laughing hysterically now, wrestling on the floor.

Digging her fingers into Sean's bony ribs, Bobbi glanced up at the clock. "Oh." She rolled away and stood up. "Come on, Corky. We've got to eat dinner and change. We'll be late for the game."

Corky gave Sean one last hard tickle, then climbed to her feet.

"Shadyside's going to lose," Sean called after them, following them downstairs. "Shadyside stinks."

The excitement of the game, the cheers of the Shadyside fans who filled the stadium, the white lights cutting through the chill of the night, making the field brighter than daylight under the starless black sky, forced all thoughts of that afternoon from Bobbi's mind.

> *"Tigers growl! Tigers roar!*
> *Do it again—more, more, MORE!"*

Across the field the Winstead High cheerleaders, in their blue and gold uniforms, were clapping and cheering, rousing the few hundred Winstead fans in the away team bleachers. Their cries barely carried over the cheers and shouts that roared down from the Shadyside supporters, and the loud blasts and drumrolls from the Shadyside marching band in their own bleachers near the end zone.

79

"Tigers roar! Tigers growl!
We want a touchdown—now, now, NOW!"

Her eyes darting back and forth from the game on the field to the crowd in the stadium, Bobbi led the girls through their cheers. They were onstage now, in full view of everyone. The bitterness and rivalries that had created so much ill feeling in practice were all forgotten.

Bobbi was in charge, and no one questioned her commands. She called out the cheers and routines they were to perform as she carefully watched the action on the field.

"Go team, go team, go-go-go-go-go GO!"

The cheers thundered down from the stadium, punctuated by applause and excited shouts. Bobbi glanced quickly down the line of cheerleaders, catching a smile of encouragement from Corky at the far end.

Before the game, Ronnie had complained that she wasn't feeling well, that she thought she was coming down with the flu. But Bobbi saw that she was giving one hundred percent, cheering with her usual enthusiasm.

At the far end of the players' bench, Bobbi spotted Jennifer. She was in her wheelchair, a maroon blanket over her lap, waving her Shadyside pennant. Their eyes met. Jennifer, smiling happily, waved. Bobbi waved back.

Whistles blew on the field. Bobbi heard laughter

spread across the stadium bleachers. She turned to see the cause of the interruption. A white wirehaired terrier had run onto the field.

Two Shadyside players were trying to chase it to the sidelines. But the dog, enjoying the attention, ran in wide circles, its stub of a tail wagging furiously.

Finally one of the referees managed to pick the dog up. He jogged to the sidelines with it to a loud chorus of good-natured boos. Then whistles rang out for the game to resume.

Bobbi stared over the heads of the players on the bench, watching Chip lead the offense out of the huddle. The first quarter had been pretty even. Both teams had been able to move the ball, although neither team had scored.

Now, as the second quarter began, the Tigers were starting on the Winstead thirty-five-yard line. Good field position. The cheers grew louder. The noise level in the stadium rose as if someone had turned up the volume control.

Watching Chip step behind the center, Bobbi wondered what he was thinking. Was he thinking about the Winstead linemen staring at him from under their helmets, about to come charging toward him? Was he thinking only about the play he had called? Was he nervous? Was he scared to death?

She decided she'd have to ask him these questions when she met him after the game.

After the game. She forced that thought out of her mind. She couldn't think about that now. She had to concentrate, stay alert, stay on the ball.

She heard Chip call out the signals in his loud, high-pitched voice. Then she saw him take the snap from center. He took a few steps back. He raised his arm to throwing position.

Another step back, his arm ready to throw.

The crowd roared. Bobbi held her breath.

Chip seemed to freeze, his arm cocked, his feet planted firmly on the grass.

He stood there until two Winstead tacklers swarmed over him and pushed him to the ground.

Bobbi realized she had been holding her breath the whole time. She exhaled, turned to the cheerleaders, and called out a clapping cheer.

What had happened to Chip? she wondered, moving in line and clapping. The crowd responded half-heartedly. The cheer was drowned out by muttering and heated voices. People in the stands must be asking the same question, she realized.

Chip had had plenty of time to throw, but he hadn't even pumped his arm. He didn't seem to be looking for a receiver. And he hadn't tried to scramble away when the line came crashing in on him.

Oh, well, thought Bobbi, it's just one play.

She and the cheerleaders finished the cheer and turned back to the game. Some of the players on the bench had climbed to their feet, so Bobbi had to move closer to see the playing field.

The stadium grew quiet as Chip stepped up to the center, quiet enough for Bobbi to hear the Winstead cheerleaders on the far side of the field.

Again, Bobbi held her breath as Chip took the ball

and stepped back. It appeared to be a running play. Dave Johnson, the Tigers' big running back, came crunching forward, his arms outstretched.

But again Chip froze in place. He didn't hand off the ball. Johnson ran past him into the line. Chip stood with the ball in his hands. He didn't run or step back to pass.

"Oh!" Bobbi cried out as Chip was tackled hard around the knees and dropped for a loss.

Voices in the stadium bleachers cried out in surprise. The entire stadium seemed to buzz. Bobbi heard a scattering of boos.

She shook her head hard as if trying to force the play from her mind. "Let's do Go Tigers," she called out.

The girls lined up quickly. Except for Kimmy, who remained just behind the players' bench, staring onto the field.

"Kimmy!" Bobbi called.

But Kimmy didn't seem to hear her. She was staring straight ahead with the strangest expression on her face.

"Kimmy!" Bobbi repeated. But it was too late to do the cheer anyway. Chip was leading the team out of the huddle for the third-down play.

Again the stadium grew quiet.

The wind suddenly picked up, blowing the flag and the big Shadyside pennant beneath it on the pole, making them flap noisily, the rope clips clanging against the metal flagpole.

Come on, Chip! Bobbi thought, crossing her fingers.

Across the field the cheerleaders in blue and gold were standing in a tight line, staring in rapt silence at the field.

Chip took the ball from the center. Johnson came rolling toward him. But Chip kept the ball. It was a fake run.

Chip backpedaled quickly and started to roll out.

"Throw it!" Bobbi screamed, cupping her hands to form a megaphone. "Throw it!"

Chip stopped.

He froze.

"Throw it! *Throw it!*"

Chip didn't move. He was holding the ball at his waist.

"Throw it!"

Shadyside players were shouting to him.

"I'm open! I'm open!" Johnson was yelling downfield.

Chip was frozen like a statue.

Bobbi's mouth dropped open in a silent cry as she saw the Winstead players close in on him.

Several tacklers got to him at the same time.

The ball dribbled out of Chip's hand as they covered him, pulled him down, and piled on top of him.

Players scrambled for the ball.

Whistles blew.

The stadium remained strangely silent.

"They *buried* him!" Bobbi heard Kimmy say.

Buried him.

Bobbi moved closer to the sidelines, stepping in front of the players' bench. The Winstead players were slowly climbing off Chip, making their way triumphantly to their bench across the field.

Buried him. Buried him.

Bobbi suddenly felt cold all over.

The tacklers were all gone now.

But Chip, sprawled flat on his back, wasn't getting up.

Chapter 13

"I Was Dead"

Bobbi showered and changed quickly into a green turtleneck sweater and a short, straight black skirt, which she pulled over green tights. She brushed her hair, frowning at herself in the water-spotted locker-room mirror.

Feeling excited, she made her way out of the room, calling out good night to the few girls who were still there. As she half-walked, half-jogged back outside to the football team's locker room, she relived that second-quarter nightmare, seeing the scene repeat in her mind.

There was Chip frozen in place. And there were the Winstead tacklers swarming over him. And there was Chip out cold on the ground, sprawled so flat, so still.

And then there came the stretcher. The worried coach and players forming a tight circle around their fallen quarterback. And then Chip being carried away. Under the bright—too bright—stadium lights, Bobbi saw his hands dangling limply, lifelessly, over the sides of the stretcher, saw that his eyes were closed, his head tilted at such a strange angle.

He's dead, she thought.

It was so silent in the stadium. So unearthly silent. We're all dead. All.

But then whistles blew. The game resumed.

"Chasner injured on the play," the stadium announcer informed everyone. Old news already.

The voices came back. The cheers and shouts. The band revived, blared out the Tigers' fight song, the tubas punctuating each beat with a raucous *blat*.

Bobbi, feeling shaken and stunned, called out the cheers. Somehow, she knew, she had to keep going.

But is he okay? she wondered.

Is he okay?

Winstead scored quickly. The Tigers came back with Overman, Chip's backup. They tried some running plays that didn't work. After three plays, they had to punt.

Again Bobbi heard scattered boos. The cheerleaders across the field were leaping high, shouting with renewed enthusiasm.

Is he okay? Is Chip okay?

The game lost all interest for her. She called out cheers, kept the routines going, all on automatic pilot.

Word on the bench was that Chip had probably suffered a mild concussion and was feeling fine now. Everyone was very relieved.

She saw that he didn't come out for the second half.

Did they take him to a hospital? Bobbi wondered. Is he still in the locker room? Does he still expect me to meet him?

The Tigers lost twenty-one to six.

And now here she was, nervously waiting in the student parking lot, in front of the door to the team dressing room. The stadium lights dimmed, then went out, casting the stadium, the parking lot, the entire back of the school, into sudden night.

As if someone had turned off the sun, Bobbi thought.

As her eyes adjusted to the new darkness, she saw Debra and Ronnie heading across the parking lot. Involved in conversation, they didn't notice her. Bobbi watched them disappear around the corner, both of them talking animatedly, gesturing with their hands.

Strange that Kimmy isn't with them, she thought. Maybe Kimmy had a date.

The locker-room door swung open. Bobbi recognized Dave Johnson, the running back. He came bouncing out, carrying a small knapsack, his hair still wet from the shower.

"Is Chip— Is he in there?" Bobbi stammered.

"Yeah. He's coming out," Johnson told her.

"Is he okay?" Bobbi asked.

But Johnson was already halfway across the rapidly emptying parking lot.

Bobbi started to shout after him, but the door opened again and Chip appeared. He moved forward unsteadily, smiling at her, his face pale, almost bloodless under the parking lot lights. He was wearing faded jeans and a Shadyside letter jacket that he had snapped up to the collar.

"Hi," he called. "How's it going?" His smile was forced, she saw. His eyes weren't quite focusing on her.

"Are you okay?" she blurted out.

The question seemed to catch him off guard. "I'm not sure," he replied, wrinkling his forehead.

He stepped closer to her.

"What happened?" Bobbi asked. "I was . . . well . . . worried."

"Me too."

She waited for him to say more, but his face fell into a thoughtful, faraway stare.

"So what happened? I mean—you're okay?"

"I guess," he said slowly. "Maybe a slight concussion. That's what they said. I'm supposed to go right home. I feel kind of funny."

"Oh." She couldn't hide the disappointment from her voice. "I have a car," she said. "Can I give you a lift?"

"Yeah. That would be great. My parents are out of town. Actually, I'm glad my mom wasn't at the game. She worries."

"Do you feel kind of weird?"

"Yeah." He nodded. "Kind of. You know, spacey."

"It looked so scary when you didn't get up," Bobbi said, leading the way to her parents' Accord, which was parked around the front on the street. "Were you knocked out?"

"I guess." He put a hand on her shoulder as if he needed to steady himself as he walked.

She slowed down. He waved to a couple of players from the team.

"Did it hurt?" she asked.

"No. Not really."

"Am I asking too many questions?" she asked.

He didn't reply.

Wow, this is sure going great, Bobbi thought unhappily. I'm asking question after question, and he's staring off into space. He can barely walk or even answer me.

They made their way in silence to the car. She unlocked the passenger door and held the door open as he slid into the front seat.

A few seconds later she started up the car and turned on the headlights. "I don't know where you live," she said, turning to him, adjusting her shoulder seat belt.

"It was like I was dead," he replied.

She stared into his eyes. "Huh?"

"It was like I was paralyzed or something. I couldn't get my body to move, to do *anything.*" He turned his eyes to the windshield. A group of kids crossed in front of the car. One of them tapped on the hood as he passed.

"Chip—are you feeling okay? Should I call your parents or something?" she asked, feeling a stab of worry in the pit of her stomach.

"Well, aren't you wondering why I didn't pass the ball? Or hand it off?" he asked heatedly. "Isn't that what everyone wants to know?"

"The doctor said you had a concussion, right?" Bobbi said, a little frightened. She started to pull away from the curb, but he stopped her, placing his hand over hers. His hand was ice-cold.

"Before I got the concussion," he said, more quietly. "Before. When I was playing. I wanted to throw the ball, but it was like I had no control. Like I was paralyzed or something. Just for that moment."

"I don't understand," Bobbi said, shaking her head.

Oncoming headlights filled the car with light. Bobbi and Chip both shielded their eyes. A car roared by filled with Shadyside kids, all the windows down, everyone singing along to a blaring radio.

"I couldn't hand it off either," Chip said. She realized he was explaining it to himself. She wondered if he even cared whether she was in the car. "I didn't freeze. I just wasn't there. I mean, I was and I wasn't. I knew where I was, but I couldn't move."

"Uh, Chip . . ." Bobbi started, reaching again for the gearshift. They still hadn't moved from the curb. "Maybe we'd better—"

He startled her by turning in the seat, leaning toward her, and grabbing her shoulders with both of his hands. "Chip—" she began.

"I'm kind of scared," he said, his eyes wild and unfocused, his face closer and closer to hers. "You know? I'm really kind of scared."

And then he pulled her down to him and started to kiss her. His lips felt hard and dry against hers. His hands held on to her shoulders, pulled her to him.

Bobbi started to pull away. But he seemed so needy, so frightened. Returning his kiss, she raised her hands to his wrists and removed them from her shoulders. Then she slid her hands around the back of his neck.

To her surprise, he was trembling all over.

The kiss ended as suddenly as it had begun. Chip, his expression a little embarrassed, leaned back against his seat. "Sorry. I—"

"That's okay," Bobbi replied, realizing her heart was pounding.

"Maybe we'd better get me home," Chip said, avoiding her eyes, staring out the passenger window, which was beginning to steam up. "I just feel so weird."

"Okay." Bobbi put the gearshift into Drive and pulled away from the curb. As he directed her to his house on Canyon Road, she repeatedly glanced over at him. He seemed to flicker on and off in the light of the passing streetlights, so pale, so ghostly pale and worried looking.

"Bobbi, what *happened* to me tonight?" he whispered, staring out of the passenger window.

Bobbi had no reply.

Chapter 14

Kimmy Has a Problem

"Bobbi—can I talk to you?"

Kimmy came bounding across the gym before practice on Monday afternoon, her cheeks flushed, her eyes angry.

"I just got here," Bobbi said distractedly, searching the gym. Everyone seemed to be ready. Megan and Heather were already working on one of the new routines. Miss Green was standing behind her desk in her office, talking on the phone.

"Sorry I'm late," Bobbi called to the others.

"I really need to talk to you," Kimmy insisted, hands on her waist. Her black crimped hair was more disheveled than usual. The sleeves of her sweater were rolled up, one above the elbow, the other below.

Bobbi waved to Corky. She tossed her backpack against the wall. "What about, Kimmy?" she asked

93

impatiently. "I've had the *worst* day. First I forgot about a chemistry quiz. Then—"

"About Chip," Kimmy said through clenched teeth.

Bobbi's eyes widened in surprise. She could feel her face growing hot. "Chip? What about him?"

Kimmy glared at her.

"Well—what about him?"

"You made a little mistake, Bobbi," Kimmy said, tapping her sneaker nervously on the gym floor, like a thumping rabbit foot. One hand played with the silver megaphone pendant she always wore around her neck.

"Huh?"

"Chip is *my* boyfriend," Kimmy said heatedly.

Bobbi glanced past Kimmy and saw that the other girls had stopped their practicing and were standing around staring with unconcealed interest at this unpleasant confrontation.

"Could we talk about this *after* practice?" Bobbi asked, gesturing to the audience they had attracted.

"No way," Kimmy insisted, fingering the silver pendant. "Chip is my boyfriend. We've been going together for a long time. Ask anyone." She gestured back to the other girls, who shifted uncomfortably and avoided Bobbi's eyes.

"Kimmy, listen—" Bobbi said quietly, backing away.

"You made a little mistake, Bobbi. A little mistake," Kimmy repeated, raising her voice, following Bobbi, moving very close to her.

Bobbi felt herself losing her temper. What right did Kimmy have to do this to her? She was only trying to embarrass Bobbi in front of the other cheerleaders.

She was only trying to turn the girls against Bobbi even more.

"You're the one who made the mistake," Bobbi blurted out. "You're forgetting one little detail, Kimmy—I didn't ask Chip out. He asked *me!"*

Kimmy's eyes grew wide. Then, uttering a cry of anger, she lunged at Bobbi, grabbing the sides of her hair with both hands, pulling hard.

Startled, Bobbi gasped. She tried to duck out of Kimmy's hold. But Kimmy had a firm grasp on her hair. Bobbi yelped in pain and struggled to pull Kimmy's hands off.

Suddenly a voice was calling, "Stop! Girls—stop! *Please!"*

And Jennifer wheeled her chair right between the two combatants. "Stop it—please! Kimmy! Bobbi!"

Both girls stumbled backward. Surprised to see Jennifer appear out of nowhere, they hesitated, panting noisily.

Bobbi's head throbbed. She raised a hand and tried to smooth her hair.

"Girls—what is going on?" Miss Green came trotting out of her office, a look of alarm on her face. "I was on the phone and when I looked up—"

"It's okay," Jennifer told her, backing her wheelchair up, her eyes on Bobbi. "A slight disagreement."

"Good Lord!" Miss Green cried, staring first at Bobbi, then at Kimmy, who had bent down to pick the silver megaphone pendant up off the floor.

Embarrassed and upset, Bobbi stared at the bleachers at the other end of the gym. Taking in big gulps of air, she struggled to catch her breath. Her throat felt as dry as cotton.

Kimmy fiddled with the clasp of the pendant chain, her hands shaking visibly. Her face was crimson, and a damp clump of her hair had fallen over one eye.

"I think you two had better apologize to each other right now," Miss Green said sternly, talking to them as if they were four-year-olds.

Neither girl replied.

Jennifer backed her wheelchair out of the way.

Kimmy fastened the megaphone pendant around her neck, glaring at Bobbi as she did it.

"This is very bad timing," Miss Green said, crossing her arms in front of her chest. "Especially since you two have to work together so closely on the new routine."

The new routine.

Bobbi had forgotten they were going to work on the new routine. She sighed. The new routine was long and difficult. And it ended with Kimmy doing a pike, diving off Corky's shoulders—and being caught by Bobbi!

"Maybe we should practice something easier today," Bobbi muttered glumly.

"We're not practicing anything until you and Kimmy apologize to each other for acting like spoiled babies," Miss Green said, frowning.

Bobbi glanced past Miss Green at the other girls. Corky was making funny faces at her. Helpful. Very helpful.

The other girls all looked terribly uncomfortable. Debra and Ronnie had gone back to practicing their splits. They were pretending that the little drama wasn't taking place.

"There's nothing to apologize about," Kimmy said defiantly.

Nothing to apologize about? Bobbi thought, rolling her eyes. She *attacked* me!

"Well, if you really feel that way," Miss Green said angrily, her arms still crossed, "I'll have no choice but to suspend both of you from the squad."

A few of the girls gasped. Ronnie and Debra stopped their exercises.

"Well . . ." Kimmy said slowly, avoiding Bobbi's eyes.

"I'm willing to apologize," Bobbi said softly. Even though this is entirely Kimmy's fault, she added to herself.

"I guess I am too," Kimmy said grudgingly, her blue eyes flashing.

"I should hope so," the advisor said, lowering her arms. "After all, this is a cheerleading squad—not the wrestling team."

Bobbi glanced at Jennifer, who had backed up nearly to the wall. Jennifer flashed Bobbi an encouraging smile.

"I'm sorry," Kimmy said sullenly, and extended her hand.

Bobbi took her hand. It felt hot and wet. "I'm sorry too," she said softly.

"That's better," Miss Green said, more than a little relieved. "I'm sure you girls can find a more civilized way to work out your differences."

Bobbi and Kimmy both nodded.

Bobbi let go of Kimmy's hand. The two eyed each other warily.

Kimmy will *never* be my friend, Bobbi realized.

Her next thought: Will she always be my enemy?

"This new routine is so tricky," Miss Green was saying, "so complicated. The timing is split-second. You two girls have to be able to rely on each other. You have to have confidence in each other." She called the other cheerleaders over to begin the practice.

Bobbi wasn't in the mood to work on anything new. She still felt strange, out of sorts. How could Kimmy have attacked her like that? Didn't she have any pride?

"Let's try the last part of the routine first," Miss Green suggested. "Why don't you explain it again, Bobbi."

"Actually, Corky should explain it," Bobbi replied, turning to her sister. "Corky invented it. We used it at the state finals last year, and it really got a big reaction."

Bobbi saw Kimmy mutter something to Debra. Both girls snickered quietly to themselves.

"It's easier to demonstrate it," Corky said. "Bobbi —do a shoulder stand. We'll do this now without the rest of the pyramid. But in the real routine, she'd be up much higher. We'll show you how the pike works. Miss Green, will you catch Bobbi when she dives?"

Bobbi and Miss Green obediently moved into place as the other girls watched intently. "You'll be doing this pike, Kimmy," Miss Green said, "so watch carefully. If you have any questions—"

"I'm watching," Kimmy said sharply.

Bobbi stepped behind Corky and grabbed Corky's hands. Then she placed one sneaker on Corky's bent knee and, with a boost from Heather, who was standing behind her, raised her other sneaker to

Corky's shoulder, and pulled herself up until she was standing on Corky's shoulders. Corky brought her hands up to Bobbi's ankles, gripping them tightly, locking her in place.

Miss Green moved in front of Corky and readied herself to catch Bobbi as she dove. "Ready, Bobbi?" Corky asked, keeping her shoulders steady, bracing herself.

"Here goes," Bobbi said. She leapt up off Corky's shoulders, bringing her feet up, folding her body into a perfect *V*, and dropped in a sitting position right into Miss Green's waiting arms.

Some of the girls burst into enthusiastic applause. "Excellent!" Miss Green cried as Bobbi lowered her feet to the floor. "You really made it look easy."

"We've practiced it a lot," Bobbi said modestly.

"Kimmy—are you ready to try it?" Miss Green asked.

"I guess so," Kimmy said reluctantly, eyeing Bobbi.

"Bobbi will catch you. Run through it slowly," Miss Green instructed as Kimmy stepped behind Corky. "Take as long as it takes. Don't worry about the number of beats. We'll practice the timing later."

The girls who were not involved in this part of the routine stepped back to make room. Ronnie was talking excitedly to two of them, shaking her head, glancing at Bobbi.

"I really don't believe this. My life is in your hands," Kimmy told Bobbi dryly.

"No problem," Bobbi replied. "I haven't dropped anyone in weeks."

Kimmy didn't smile at Bobbi's joke. Corky braced herself. Kimmy pulled herself up quickly into a standing position on her shoulders. Corky grabbed her calves to brace her.

Bobbi moved into position to catch Kimmy. "I'm ready whenever you are," she called up to her.

"Shouldn't she go on a diet first?" Debra cracked.

Kimmy glared down at her. "Since when do *you* make jokes?"

Debra shrugged. "Ronnie made me say it."

"Let's get serious, girls," Miss Green scolded. "This stunt could really be dangerous."

"Corky and I have done it a million times," Bobbi reassured her, looking up at Kimmy. "Ready?"

"I guess," Kimmy replied with a shrug. "Wish I had a safety net."

"You can do it!" Jennifer yelled encouragement from against the wall.

"Okay. On three," Corky said. "One, two—"

Bobbi braced herself, spreading her feet far apart in preparation for the catch. She arched her back. And started to raise both arms above her head.

"—three!"

Bobbi sucked in a mouthful of air. My arms, she thought. What's wrong? What's happening to me?

I can't raise my arms, Bobbi thought, frozen in horror.

I can't move. I can't move anything.

She could feel beads of cold sweat run down her forehead.

Stop! Bobbi thought. You've got to stop this! Hold everything! Please! Just stop!

But to her horror, she couldn't speak out. She couldn't make a sound.

I can't move. I can't speak.

She strained to raise her arms, to get into position.

No! Please—no! Bobbi cried, only no **sound came out.**

What is happening to me?

She could see herself standing there, as if she had floated out of her own body.

She could see herself looking up as Kimmy prepared to dive, looking up with her arms still at her sides.

Unable to move them, to raise them.

Unable to catch Kimmy.

Unable to warn her.

No! Please—Kimmy, don't dive! Don't dive!

Can't you see I'm paralyzed here?

Can't you see something is holding me here? Holding me in its grip? Holding me so I can't move a single muscle, cannot even blink?

Can't you see?

Corky's shoulders bobbed under Kimmy's weight as Kimmy bent her knees and began her jump.

No! No! Kimmy—don't!

Kimmy's eyes narrowed, her features tight in intent concentration. Her knees bent, the muscles tightened.

No! Stop!

Kimmy—stop!

I can't catch you!

I can't even move to break your fall.

Kimmy—please!

Kimmy took a deep breath. Held it.

And then she leapt off Corky's shoulders.

Chapter 15

The Accusations Fly

Kimmy hit the floor hard.

She landed first on her knees and elbows.

Everyone heard a sickening crack. And then a heavy thud as her forehead smashed against the floor.

Her head snapped back and her mouth let out a *whoosh*, like air escaping a blown-out tire.

And then her eyes closed, and she didn't move.

At first no one reacted. Everyone seemed as paralyzed as Bobbi.

But then Heather's shrill scream pierced the air, echoing off the high gym ceiling.

Several other girls cried out.

Corky dropped to her knees beside Kimmy's unmoving body and stared up at Bobbi.

Her eyes locked on Kimmy, Bobbi stumbled back. One step. Two.

She raised her hands to her cheeks.

I can move, she realized.

I can move again.

I'm *me* again.

Jennifer was wheeling her chair frantically toward Kimmy.

Miss Green leaned over Kimmy, took her hand, slapped at it.

Kimmy groaned.

"She had the wind knocked out," Miss Green announced. She raised her eyes to the girls huddling around the fallen cheerleader. "Quick—call for an ambulance. Call nine-one-one."

Megan and Heather, pale and shaken, went racing from the gym.

I can move now, Bobbi thought. But what happened to me?

"You didn't *try* to catch her!" Debra's words stung Bobbi. Stepping close, Debra pointed an accusing finger. "You didn't even *try!*"

"No—" Bobbi didn't know what to say. She took a step back, away from Debra's accusing finger.

"You just let her fall!" Ronnie cried shrilly. She had tears running down her cheeks.

"No!" Bobbi cried. "I tried, but—"

"You didn't try!" Ronnie screamed. "We saw you. We all saw you!"

"You just *stood* there!" Debra cried angrily.

"It was deliberate," Ronnie said. "She did it deliberately."

Corky, still on her knees beside Kimmy, stared up at her sister. "What happened?" She mouthed the words silently.

"I couldn't catch her," Bobbi explained, knowing how lame her words sounded. "My arms—"

Bobbi stopped. It didn't make any sense to *her*. How could she make it make sense to *them*?

"You were mad at her. So you let her fall," Ronnie accused.

"How *could* you?" Debra cried.

Kimmy stirred and opened her eyes.

"You had the wind knocked out of you," Miss Green said softly, still holding her hand.

Kimmy groaned. Her eyes darted from face to face. "My arm," she groaned.

"Your arm?" Miss Green lowered Kimmy's hand to the floor.

"The other one," Kimmy groaned. "I can't move it. I think it's—"

"We heard a crack," Miss Green said. "Maybe you broke it."

Kimmy tried to raise herself.

"No." Miss Green pushed her gently back down. "Don't try to get up. There's an ambulance on the way."

"Ohhh, it hurts." Kimmy stared up at Bobbi. "You—you did this to me. On purpose," she said, her voice a pained whisper.

"No!" Bobbi protested.

"You just let me fall," Kimmy accused, wincing from the pain in her arm.

"Lie back," Miss Green instructed her. "You're going to be okay, dear. You're going to be just fine. Don't worry about Bobbi now, okay?" She glanced up at Bobbi, and her expression became hard and cold.

"Bobbi and I will be having a good, long talk. Bobbi has a lot of explaining to do."

"I'm sure it was an accident," Corky said, suddenly bursting into the conversation. "We've done this dive a million times. Really."

"She tried to hurt her," Debra insisted. "I watched her the whole time."

"It's attempted murder!" she heard Ronnie tell Megan, deliberately loud enough for Bobbi to hear.

"Ronnie—you're going too far!" Miss Green scolded.

"We *saw* her!" Ronnie shot back angrily.

"No!" Bobbi screamed, tugging at the sides of her hair. "No! No! NO!"

She couldn't take any more of this.

She couldn't take the eyes, so many eyes, staring at her with so much hatred.

She couldn't take the accusing frowns, the pointing fingers.

She couldn't take the sting of their words.

"No! No!"

And without realizing it, she had turned away from them, away from their eyes, away from their hatred. And now she was running, her sneakers loud against the hard floor, running blindly, her eyes blurred by hot tears, running with her arms outstretched, running to the double doors.

And pushing through them. Into the coolness of the hallway. Out of the heat, away from their eyes, their unforgiving eyes.

She turned and ran toward the stairs. Past the white-coated paramedics hurrying toward the gym, carrying a stretcher and black bags of equipment. Past a surprised group of students gathered in the middle of the hall.

Up the stairs and out of the building, without stopping for her jacket, without stopping for her books.

Out into the cold, gray afternoon. Her sneakers crunching over dead leaves, hot tears stinging her eyes.

She ran as fast as her heart was pounding.

She just wanted to run forever.

But then two hands grabbed her roughly from behind.

Bobbi gasped and flailed out with both hands.

"No—don't!" she cried.

Chapter 16

Strange Shadows

"Bobbi—what's wrong?"

Chip let go of her shoulders and backed away, startled by her wild reaction.

"Oh. Chip. I—" The words caught in her throat.

"I'm sorry. I didn't mean to scare you," he said, his eyes studying her, his expression alarmed. "I saw you running and—"

"Chip—it happened to me too!" Bobbi blurted out, half-talking, half-crying. She grabbed the sleeve of his letter jacket, pressed her face against it.

"Huh? Where's your coat? Aren't you cold?"

"It happened to me too," she repeated, not recognizing her shrill, frightened voice. She straightened up, saw that her tears had run onto his jacket sleeve. "I—I couldn't move."

"You? Really?" Chip stared at her, as if he didn't

quite know what to make of her words, as if he didn't understand. Or didn't believe her. "I'm going to the doctor's. For tests. Right now," he said awkwardly. "I was just telling Coach I had to miss practice. He said—"

"I couldn't move," Bobbi repeated, as if repeating it would make him believe her. "I couldn't raise my arms. Just like you, Chip."

She stared into his eyes imploringly.

"You should get to a doctor too," he said softly. "Mine thinks it's some kind of muscle thing. These tests—"

A horn honked loudly, insistently, behind them.

"Hey—that's my brother. He's taking me to the doctor," Chip said, turning to wave to the driver. "I've got to go."

"Can I call you later?" Bobbi asked. "I mean, I've really got to talk to you. About . . . what happened."

"Yeah. Sure," he said, jogging to the car. "I'll be home later." He stopped suddenly and turned back to her. "You need a lift?"

"No." She shook her head. "I want to walk. Thanks."

He climbed into the passenger seat. The car sped off.

He's the only one who will believe me, Bobbi thought, watching the car until it disappeared around the next corner.

He's the only one.

It happened to him too. I'm not cracking up. I'm *not*.

* * *

"I'm not cracking up," she told Jennifer. "It happened to Chip too."

Jennifer's eyes flared for a brief second when Bobbi mentioned Chip's name. She wheeled herself back against the wall, giving Bobbi room to pass her and enter the den.

"Thanks for letting me come over," Bobbi said gratefully. She tossed her backpack onto the floor beside a couch and started to pull off her coat. "My parents took my little brother to a Cub Scout dinner, and Corky is baby-sitting tonight. I just didn't want to be alone."

"That was so awful this afternoon," Jennifer said, speaking slowly, cautiously. "You must have felt terrible." She wheeled herself back into the den, banging into the frame of the narrow doorway, backing up, and succeeding on the second try.

Bobbi dropped her coat on top of her backpack and rubbed the sleeves of her blue, long-sleeved pullover to warm herself. "Yeah. I—I was—" She stopped, unable to describe how she had felt.

"So did you talk to Chip about it?" Jennifer asked.

"I—I tried to call him. There was no answer. No one at his house."

"Would you like some tea?" Jennifer asked softly. "You look chilled."

"No. No, thanks. Maybe later," Bobbi said. "Do *you* believe me, Jen? Do *you* believe that I didn't deliberately let Kimmy fall?"

"I talked to her mother," Jennifer replied, avoiding the question. "She has a broken wrist. It's in a cast. But it's her left hand, so it isn't so bad."

"Do you believe me?" Bobbi demanded, sitting on the edge of the couch, leaning forward expectantly, her hands clasped nervously in front of her.

"I really don't know what to believe," Jennifer replied reluctantly.

"It was like someone was holding me down, holding me in place, smothering me. My arms were useless," Bobbi said, explaining for the hundredth time. "Useless. My whole body was useless."

"I know what *that's* like," Jennifer said with sudden bitterness. She stared down at her legs.

"Oh, Jen—I'm *sorry!*" Bobbi cried, jumping to her feet, feeling her face grow hot. "That was so *thoughtless* of me. I—"

Jennifer gestured for her to sit back down. "You've had a hard day, Bobbi. A horrible day."

"Do you think Miss Green will let me stay on the squad?" Bobbi asked, dropping back onto the couch.

Jennifer shrugged. "Do you want to try to study or something? Take your mind off what happened?"

Bobbi sighed. "I don't know if I *can* take my mind off it."

"Let's try," Jennifer said, tossing her beautiful, wavy hair behind her shoulders. "I'll make us some tea, and we'll try."

Jennifer tried valiantly, but she couldn't rouse Bobbi from her frightened, unhappy thoughts. No matter what they talked about, Bobbi's mind trailed back to the gym, back to her mysterious, terrifying paralysis, back to Kimmy's plunge to the floor.

Again and again, Bobbi heard the *crack* of Kimmy's wrist breaking. She heard the *thud* of Kimmy's forehead hitting the floorboards, saw Kimmy's head snap back and her eyes close.

Again and again, she saw the accusing eyes of the other cheerleaders and heard their outraged cries.

A little after eleven o'clock, Bobbi glumly pulled on her jacket, hoisted her backpack to a shoulder, and headed for the front door. "Thanks for keeping me company," she told Jennifer, and leaned down to give her friend a hug.

"Any time," Jennifer replied with a yawn.

"Where are *your* parents?" Bobbi asked.

"Visiting some friends," Jennifer said sleepily. "They'll probably be home soon."

"Well, thanks again," Bobbi said, pulling open the front door, feeling the chill of the night air against her hot face. "See you tomorrow, Jen."

"Get some sleep" were Jennifer's parting words. She wheeled herself to the door.

Bobbi closed the door behind her. She looked out into a dark, starless night. The air was cold and wet. From the driveway she could see a white covering of frost on her car windshield, reflecting off the street-light.

Shivering, she made her way down the drive, her high-tops crunching over the gravel.

Crunch, crunch, she thought. Like the crunch of bones.

When she got down to the car, she rubbed a finger over the frost on the windshield. It wasn't very frozen. She didn't need to scrape it off. The windshield wipers would take care of it.

She pulled open the car door. Then, before climbing behind the wheel, she glanced back at the house.

And gasped.

"Whoa!" she exclaimed out loud, her breath steamy white in front of her as she squinted at the large living-room picture window.

It was the only lighted window in the front of the house. A window shade had been pulled down, covering the entire window. The bright living-room lights made the shade bright orange and cast shadows onto it.

Moving shadows.

Squinting hard, Bobbi realized that she was seeing Jennifer's shadow against the shade.

And Jennifer was walking.

Pacing back and forth in front of the window.

"Whoa," Bobbi repeated.

She blinked several times.

But when she reopened her eyes and directed them back to the window, the shadow didn't change or fade away.

Jennifer, Bobbi knew, was the only one home. And Jennifer was out of her wheelchair. Jennifer was walking!

"What's going on?" Bobbi asked out loud.

I'm definitely cracking up, she decided. I've got to get help. I'm seeing things.

She took a step up the driveway. Then another. Her sneakers slid over the wet gravel.

I'm crazy. Crazy. Crazy.

But, no. As she drew closer to the house, the gray shadow against the orange shade continued to move steadily back and forth. The image grew clearer. Sharper.

It was Jennifer. She was *walking,* her hands knotted in front of her.

What's going on? Bobbi wondered, her mind whirring with wild ideas.

Is it a miracle? Did Jennifer just this second discover she could walk?

No. That wasn't likely. Then . . .

Has Jennifer been faking all along?

Why? Why would she fake paralysis?

Why?

Bobbi stepped back onto the stoop. She rang the doorbell.

She had to know. She had to ask Jennifer what was going on.

She leaned toward the door and listened for Jennifer's footsteps.

Silence.

She rang the bell again.

Finally the front door was pulled open, revealing a widening rectangle of light.

"Jennifer!" Bobbi cried.

Chapter 17

Cracking Up

S tanding on the front stoop, Bobbi stared into the yellow light of the front hallway. Jennifer held the door open, her face filled with surprise.

"Bobbi—what's the matter?"

"Oh . . . uh . . ." Bobbi stammered. "Nothing. I . . . thought I forgot my gloves."

Jennifer's face relaxed. She settled back in her wheelchair. She wheeled herself back a few inches, still gripping the doorknob. "Do you want to come in and look for them?"

"No," Bobbi replied quickly. "I just remembered I didn't bring any gloves. Sorry."

Jennifer laughed. "You're really in a state, aren't you?"

"Yeah. I guess." Bobbi felt totally embarrassed. And confused.

And worried.

Jennifer was in her wheelchair, a small blanket over her lap. Why had Bobbi imagined that she'd seen her pacing back and forth across the window?

Had Bobbi imagined it all, imagined the moving shadow, imagined the dark figure walking across the living room?

What's *wrong* with me? Bobbi asked herself, saying good night to Jennifer again and trudging back down the gravel driveway.

Her breath rose in puffs of white steam against the cold night air.

But Bobbi didn't feel the cold.

In fact, she felt hot. Feverish. Her forehead throbbed, a sharp pain just behind her eyes.

Why am I seeing things?

Am I seeing things?

Am I cracking up? Really cracking up?

The headlights seemed to skip and dance as she drove through the silent darkness back to her house on Fear Street. The house was dark except for the porch light. She realized everyone must have gone to bed.

Tossing her jacket onto the banister, she hurried up to her bedroom and, without turning on the light, shook Corky awake.

"Huh?" Corky cried out, frightened, and sat up stiffly.

"It's me," Bobbi whispered. "Wake up."

"You scared me to death!" Corky cried angrily. She never liked to be awakened.

Bobbi clicked on the bedside lamp. "I saw Jennifer walk!" she blurted out.

Corky yawned. "Huh?"

"I think I saw Jennifer walk. I'm not sure, but—"

"What time is it?" Corky asked crankily. "You must have been dreaming."

"No. I wasn't asleep," Bobbi insisted. "I was standing outside her house. I saw shadows."

Corky stretched, turned, and lowered her feet to the floor. She brushed a strand of blond hair from over her eyes. "You saw shadows?" Her face filled with concern. "Bobbi, I'm really worried about you."

"No! Really! I saw her," Bobbi said, not realizing that she was almost shouting. She stood over her sister, her hands knotted tensely in front of her, feeling hot and trembly, the pain still pulsing behind her eyes.

"Maybe we should tell Mom and Dad," Corky said, glancing at the bedside clock. "I mean, just stop and think for a minute, Bobbi. First you told me you saw all the lockers at school open and close when you walked down the hall. Then you told me you were paralyzed at practice this afternoon. You couldn't move. You couldn't even speak. And that's why you let Kimmy fall."

"But, Corky—"

"Let me finish," Corky said sharply, holding up a hand as if to fend Bobbi off. "Then there was that weird story about Chip, about how he froze, too, and couldn't move. And now you come home from Jennifer's and—"

"But it's *true!*" Bobbi cried. "It's all true. I mean, I *think* it's true. I think—I— Don't you *believe* me, Corky?"

Corky was holding her hands over her ears. "Stop shouting. You're screaming right in my face."

"Sorry. I—"

"Let's go tell everything to Mom and Dad," Corky urged. "I really think you have to go talk to a doctor or something. I think you need help, Bobbi. I really do."

"You don't believe me," Bobbi accused heatedly, bitterly, her head throbbing. "You don't believe me."

Without thinking about it, she picked up Corky's pillow and heaved it at her angrily.

"Hey—" Corky cried, grabbing the pillow and tossing it back in its place.

"Just don't talk to me!" Bobbi snapped. "Traitor!"

"Oh, fine!" Corky screamed. "That's just fine with me! You're crazy, Bobbi! Crazy!"

Bobbi stormed over to the closet. "Shut up! Just shut up! Don't talk to me! Ever again!" She began to tear off her clothes, tossing them on the closet floor, muttering to herself.

Corky punched her pillow, fluffed it, and slid back under the covers, turning her back on her sister.

She's gone totally crazy, she told herself. She's just so weird!

Imagine—calling me a traitor because I think she should talk to someone and get help.

Me, a traitor.

And now she's gotten me so upset, I'll probably be up all night.

I hate her. I really hate her, Corky thought darkly, struggling to get comfortable. She just makes me so mad.

* * *

Corky might have been more sympathetic. She might have been more understanding. More caring. More believing.

But Corky had no way of knowing that this was the last night she would ever spend with her sister.

PART THREE

The Evil

Chapter 18

In Hot Water

"Okay, everyone—some aerobics to warm up!"

Bobbi trotted enthusiastically onto the gym floor, clapping her hands, trying to get the girls up for their after-school practice.

But they lingered against the wall, clustered in pairs, talking quietly.

"Come on, everyone—line up! Let's warm up!"

Bobbi's eyes wandered from girl to girl. Where's Corky? she wondered, and then remembered that Corky had to stay late in Mr. Grant's science lab. She saw Jennifer wheel herself in, concentrating as she maneuvered her wheelchair through the double doors. Jennifer saw Bobbi and smiled, giving her a little wave.

"Line up!" Bobbi insisted.

"Where's Miss Green?" Kimmy asked, stepping forward slowly, holding her wrist with the white cast on it awkwardly.

"I don't know," Bobbi told her. "Are you going to warm up with us? Or does your wrist—"

"My wrist is no concern of yours," Kimmy snapped. "I'm not quitting the squad because of it, if that's what you mean." Her eyes burned angrily into Bobbi's.

"Let's warm up! Come on, everyone!" Bobbi called out, ignoring Kimmy's anger.

Slowly the girls moved away from the wall and formed a line in front of Bobbi. Bobbi started up the tape player. They began their aerobic exercises, the same routine they had followed since school began.

But they performed halfheartedly, grudgingly, without enthusiasm.

"Come on—let's work up a sweat!" Bobbi cried, working doubly hard, as if to make up for their feeble effort. But the girls ignored her. Debra and Ronnie, she saw, were carrying on a conversation while going through the motions.

Bobbi glanced toward the wall. Jennifer gave her a thumbs-up, but it didn't cheer her. The girls, she knew, were deliberately not cooperating.

She stopped the music. "Let's work on Steam Heat," she suggested. "Ronnie, do you want to take the end this time?"

"Huh?"

"Do you want to take the end? You can lead it."

"I don't know." Ronnie shrugged. "Whatever." She turned back to her conversation with Debra.

Without Corky, I don't have anyone on my side,

Bobbi realized, suddenly overcome by a powerful wave of depression. Only Jennifer, I guess. But even she doesn't want to speak up for me in front of the girls—not after what happened to Kimmy.

"Okay, line up for Steam Heat," Bobbi called out, struggling to keep up a show of enthusiasm.

"I think we should wait for Miss Green," Kimmy said defiantly.

"Yeah. Let's wait," Debra added quickly.

"No reason to wait," Bobbi said unsteadily. She glanced up at the scoreboard clock. Three forty-five. "We know what we have to work on, don't we?"

"I still think we should wait," Kimmy said, a definite challenge to Bobbi's authority.

"Yeah. Wait," Debra muttered nastily. Heather and Megan nodded in sullen agreement.

It's a mutiny, Bobbi realized, suddenly dizzy.

"Line up!" she insisted, glancing at Jennifer, whose smile had faded. She was watching the proceedings with a look of concern. "Kimmy, if you have something to say to me—" Bobbi started.

"I think Miss Green has something to say to you," Kimmy replied smugly. Beside her, Ronnie snickered out loud.

The double doors swung open, and Miss Green entered, taking long, rapid strides, carrying a bulging briefcase. "Sorry I'm late," she called out, heading to her office in the corner.

Seeing them on the floor, Bobbi by herself in front of the sullen-looking group, Miss Green stopped. "You've started?"

"Not exactly," Kimmy told her, shooting Bobbi a meaningful glance.

"No one seems to be in the mood to work today," Bobbi reported reluctantly.

Miss Green shifted the heavy briefcase to her other hand. "Bobbi—could I see you in my office for a minute?"

"Yeah, sure," Bobbi replied, dread building in the pit of her stomach, her throat tightening.

"Everyone—let's cancel practice for today, okay?" Miss Green said, her eyes on Kimmy.

Uh-oh, Bobbi thought. She could feel the blood pulsing at her temples.

"We'll regroup tomorrow afternoon," Miss Green said.

Talking quietly among themselves, the cheerleaders obediently moved off the floor and began to collect their belongings. Bobbi realized that all of them were avoiding looking at her. She caught a smug grin on Kimmy's face, but Kimmy quickly turned her head and walked away with Debra and Ronnie.

They all know what Miss Green is going to say to me, Bobbi realized.

And I know too.

As the gym quickly emptied out, Bobbi followed Miss Green to her office, her heart pounding, her legs suddenly feeling as if they weighed a thousand pounds.

Miss Green dropped the briefcase onto her desk. She sifted through a few pink phone-message sheets, then looked up at Bobbi. "Health forms," she said, patting the briefcase. "They weigh a ton. You've got to be strong to be in the phys. ed. department."

Bobbi stood awkwardly in front of the desk, nervously toying with a strand of her hair. When Miss Green motioned her toward a seat, Bobbi obediently lowered herself into it, folding her hands in her lap.

She realized she was perspiring. It was so hot in the gym, and she had been the only one to really work during the aerobics warm-ups.

"Bobbi, I'm really sorry," Miss Green said abruptly, setting down the pink message sheets and leaning with both hands on the desktop. "I have to ask you to step down from the squad."

"Oh!" Bobbi uttered a short cry.

She had anticipated those very words. But somehow they had come as a surprise anyway.

"I really don't—" she started.

Miss Green held up a hand to silence her. "I don't want to discuss what happened yesterday. I know you wouldn't deliberately try to injure one of the girls. But what happened, happened. Whether it was a loss of concentration or whatever. It happened."

She sat down, leaning forward over the desk, playing with an opal ring on her right hand. "You're a very talented cheerleader, Bobbi," she continued. "You and your sister. I like you both. But after yesterday, I'm afraid—well, I'm afraid you've lost the confidence of the squad."

"Confidence?" Bobbi managed to utter in a tight, choked voice. She suddenly realized she was breathing hard. Drops of perspiration were sliding down her forehead, but she made no attempt to wipe them away.

"A squad is built on trust. And the girls just don't feel they can trust you," Miss Green said, lowering her voice, her face expressionless. "They've made it very clear to me. Whether it's true or not, *they* believe that you deliberately didn't catch Kimmy yesterday." She cleared her throat noisily, covering her mouth with one hand. "I'm really sorry, Bobbi. I have no choice. I have to ask you to quit."

Bobbi lowered her head, struggling to stop her body from shaking, struggling to hold back her tears. "I understand," she managed to whisper.

"If you'd like to talk to someone," Miss Green offered, her eyes sympathetic, "a doctor, I mean. If you'd like me to recommend someone you could . . . confide in—"

Bobbi rose to her feet. She had to get out of there, she realized. She felt hot and cold and shaky and sick. "No, thanks. I'll just leave now," she said, turning to the door, avoiding Miss Green's stare.

"I know how you must feel," Miss Green said, standing too. "If there's anything I can do . . ."

A few seconds later Bobbi found herself in the locker room. Alone. Her footsteps echoing on the damp concrete floor. She choked back a sob.

I'm wringing wet. Wringing wet.

I'll take a shower, she decided. Change into street clothes.

That'll make me feel better.

She thought she heard a scraping sound from another row of lockers. "Anybody here?" she called in a quivery voice.

No reply.

"Now I'm *hearing* things too," she said out loud.

Oh, well, she thought, pulling her sweatshirt over her head, at least now I'll have more time to study.

126

With that thought, the sob she'd been holding back burst out.

How could this *happen* to me? How could this happen?

Am I really going crazy?

Leaving her clothes on the bench, she pulled a towel from her locker and padded over the damp floor toward the shower room. A warm shower would be soothing, she decided. She'd make it nice and hot. It would stop the trembling, stop the chills down her back.

She turned at the entrance to the showers, thinking she heard someone again. She listened. Again, silence.

She stepped into the large shower room with its stained tile walls, its row of chrome shower heads. The floor was puddled with cold water, left over from last-period gym class.

Bobbi shivered.

I'm so cold. So cold.

As she reached up to turn on the water, metal doors nearby slammed shut with a *clang*.

"Huh?"

At first Bobbi wasn't sure what had happened. She jumped, startled by the loud, unexpected noise. Maybe someone had entered the dressing area outside, she decided.

But then she saw that the shower room doors had been closed.

That's weird, she thought. She turned on the water.

And screamed as scalding water burst out of the shower head with a roar, striking her chest, her shoulders.

"Ow!"

She dodged away. But the next shower head was spraying down hot water, too, scalding hot, burning hot.

"Help!"

All the showers were turned on now. Scalding hot water shooting out of all of them.

Something's wrong, Bobbi realized, stumbling back in a panic, her chest burning, her legs burning. Something's terribly wrong.

"Ow!"

She slipped and toppled backward, landing with a splash in a steaming puddle.

"Help!"

Scrambling to her feet, she saw that the hot water was rising rapidly. The drain appeared to be clogged.

"Ow!"

The water was nearly an inch deep already, and so hot, it burned her feet.

The steam rose like a thick, choking curtain.

Gasping in the hot, wet air, Bobbi lunged for the doors. She tugged on the handles. "Hey—" They wouldn't move.

"Hey—"

She struggled to push open the doors. But they were stuck. Or blocked. Or locked.

"Hey—!"

The steam was thick. She felt as if her lungs were burning, filling up. It was so hard to breathe.

Crying out from the pain of the scalding water, she hopped back to the wall of shower heads, reached for the first control knob, turned it, turned, turned. . . .

To her horror the water didn't slow. Didn't grow colder.

Frantically she turned another knob. Another. Another.

"Ow!"

She couldn't shut them off.

"I can't *breathe!*" The steam was so thick, so hot. "I can't *see!*"

She slipped, stumbling back to the double doors.

"Help me!" She choked out a desperate cry. "Somebody—help!"

The water was up over her ankles. Why wouldn't it drain? She danced wildly, a dance of unbearable pain.

"Help me! I can't—breathe!"

The rush of water became a roar.

She closed her eyes and covered her ears.

The roar didn't go away.

The pain didn't go away.

The roar grew louder.

Then all was silence.

Chapter 19

What Corky Found

Where'd everyone go? Corky wondered.

She stepped into the gym, shifting her backpack to her other shoulder. "Anyone here?" she called, her voice echoing against the high ceiling.

Her sneakers squeaked on the shiny, polished floor. She glanced up at the scoreboard clock. Not even four-thirty.

Practice usually lasted until five, she knew.

So where *was* everyone?

Had they moved the practice outdoors? Sometimes they did that on nice days. It was good to practice in the stadium, get some fresh air, get out of the gym, which was usually stifling hot.

But it was gray and blustery outside today, not a day for an outdoor practice.

Her footsteps echoed as she made her way to Miss

Green's office and peered in through the big glass window.

Empty. The papers all neatly stacked on one corner of the desk. The chair pushed in.

I guess practice ended early for some reason, Corky thought, shaking her head.

Well, Bobbi must be glad. She wasn't in any mood to face the girls anyway.

Bobbi. I wanted to talk to her, to make up, Corky thought.

She pushed open the door to the locker room and stuck her head inside. "Bobbi? Anyone?"

The locker room seemed empty too.

She was about to close the door when she heard the sound of rushing water.

Someone's taking a shower, she decided.

She made her way into the locker room, warmer and steamier than usual. Through a row of lockers.

She spotted someone's clothes tossed onto one of the long benches that stretched in front of the lockers. On the other side of the lockers, she could hear the rush of shower water going full force. She picked up the sweatshirt, recognized it as Bobbi's.

So Bobbi was taking a shower.

By herself?

Where were the other girls?

This didn't make any sense.

Corky took a step toward the shower room, then stopped. She had spotted something on the floor under Bobbi's things. Something shiny.

She bent down and picked it up, bringing it up close to her face to examine it. It was Kimmy's silver pendant, the shiny little megaphone.

It must have fallen off again, Corky decided. She rolled it into a tissue and stuffed it into the pocket of her jeans.

I'll have to remember to return it to her.

She walked past the lockers, turned toward the shower room, then stopped in surprise. The shower doors were closed.

Weird, she thought.

The shower doors were *never* closed. She didn't even know they *could* close.

As Corky drew nearer, the rush of water on the other side of the door grew louder. Could one shower make all that noise? she wondered.

She knocked on the metal door. "Hey—Bobbi!"

No reply.

"Bobbi?" She pounded harder.

She can't hear me over the water, Corky decided.

She put a hand on each of the two door handles and pulled.

The doors swung open easily.

"Hey—!" Corky shrieked as a tidal wave of hot water came spewing out at her. "Whoa!"

Startled, she staggered back until she bumped into the side of a locker. The hot water rolled over her sneakers, washed up onto the legs of her jeans.

"Ow! Hey—" It was boiling hot.

She looked up to see thick, white steam floating into the locker room, like a fog rolling over a beach.

What's going on? she wondered, more angry than frightened. Who closed the doors?

Where is Bobbi?

The steaming hot water flooded through the locker room, but it sounded as if the water had been shut off.

Walking on tiptoe, Corky made her way back to the shower room.

Holding on to the tile wall, she peered inside, squinting against the swirling steam.

And saw Bobbi.

Lying facedown against the wall under the shower heads.

"Bobbi—?"

Through gaps in the parting fog, her body slowly became visible.

Her arms were crumpled beneath her. Her legs were folded. Her hair was soaked and matted over her head and onto the floor.

Her back, her legs, her skin—her entire body was as red as a lobster.

"Bobbi—?"

Gripped with fear, Corky plunged into the room, dropped to her knees in the scalding water.

"Bobbi—?"

With a loud gasp, she reached down and pulled her sister's head up by the hair.

"Bobbi—? Bobbi—? Please?"

Bobbi stared back at her with vacant, wide-eyed terror, her flesh swollen and red, her mouth locked open in a silent scream.

"Bobbi—?"

No. No answer.

The heavy steam settled over Corky, making her shiver.

Holding her sister tightly in her arms, Corky knew that Bobbi would never answer her again.

Chapter 20

Corky Figures It Out

A pearly full moon seemed to hover over the Fear Street cemetery, casting pale, ghostly light over the jagged tombstones. Trees whispered and shook their nearly leafless branches in the cold, gusting wind.

Corky slipped on wet leaves, and she nearly lost her balance. A light rain had just ended, leaving the weed-choked ground between the graves soft and muddy.

Like quicksand, she thought. She had a sudden picture of sinking into the ground, of being pulled down, down, until only her head poked out. And then it too would be sucked into the mud to join the corpses.

Something slithered through the clump of dead leaves near her feet. A squirrel? A mouse?

Even in a graveyard, there are living things, she thought. She shivered and dug her bare hands deeper into her coat pockets.

The wind died down as she made her way along the path through the old section of graves. Bobbi was buried in a new section up a little hill, away from the street. Corky knew the way well.

The old tombstones, poking up from the ground like rotting teeth, cast long shadows on the ground at Corky's feet. At the end of the first row, she stopped. Why did the stone on the end look familiar?

Creeping closer, her boots sinking into the mud, Corky read the inscription: SARAH FEAR. 1875–1899.

"Sarah Fear," Corky said aloud, staring at the carved name. She suddenly remembered. This was the grave that Jennifer had been found sprawled on, on that horrible night she had been thrown from the bus.

"Sarah Fear."

And what were these four stones behind Sarah Fear's grave?

Moving closer, Corky leaned down to read the low stones. The names had been worn off over the years. But the dates were clearly readable. They had all died in the same year: 1899.

Four grave markers with the same year that Sarah Fear had died.

What had happened? Corky wondered. Had Sarah Fear's entire family been wiped out at once?

People died so young back then, Corky thought, climbing back to her feet. Sarah Fear would have been only twenty-four.

Without realizing it, she uttered a loud sob.

Bobbi was only seventeen.

Hands shoved in her jacket pockets, Corky turned away from the old graves and made her way along the familiar path up to the new section.

The wind picked up again, cold and wet. She could hear a dog howling mournfully somewhere down the block. The trees shivered their wintry limbs. Dead leaves scattered as if trying to flee.

"Here I am again," Corky said, placing a hand on top of her sister's temporary marker. "You're probably getting tired of seeing me."

How many times had Corky visited her sister's grave since the funeral two weeks before? Nearly every day?

"I just miss you so much," Corky whispered, holding on to the cold marker, feeling the tears well up in her eyes.

She thought about the funeral, saw it all again. The flowers, so bright and colorful and out of place on that gray, mournful day. Her parents, holding hands, leaning against each other, hiding their faces so outsiders couldn't see their pain.

Again, Corky saw the cheerleaders, huddled together, silent and pale. Jennifer stayed by herself in the wheelchair, a wool blanket over her legs, tears trickling down her cheeks.

Chip had been there too, looking awkward and uncomfortable. He had been nice to Corky, tried to say something comforting, but ended up stammering about how sorry he was and hurrying off.

And Kimmy. Kimmy had been there too. Standing a little way off from the other cheerleaders, her arms crossed tightly in front of her, her expression grim, unchanging, her eyes on Chip.

A cold drizzle had begun to fall when they lowered Bobbi's coffin into the ground. Corky felt her mother's arms go around her and Sean. They were all weeping, she realized, their tears dropping into the open grave.

Corky had looked up through tear-clouded eyes to see Kimmy again, still staring at Chip. And then, as the drizzle turned to a hard, steady rain, people started to leave, pushing up their coat collars, ducking under black umbrellas.

Jennifer's father appeared and wheeled her away. Chip had hurried off, taking long, awkward strides over the mud. Kimmy left with the other cheerleaders, their heads lowered, bent against the wind and rain.

Corky and her family were left alone.

Without Bobbi.

Without Bobbi forever.

And now it was two weeks later, and Corky still couldn't get used to the idea that she no longer had her sister to talk to.

"I'm back again," Corky said, turning her eyes up to the full moon. "I know you can hear me, Bobbi. I—I just wish you could answer."

Her next words caught in her throat. She stopped, took a deep breath, taking in the sweet, cold air.

"I just wanted to tell you the news," she continued after a long pause. "They made Kimmy captain of the cheerleaders. You probably guessed that would happen, right? Well, everyone seems real happy about it. Especially Kimmy. The news sure made her wrist get better in a hurry."

Corky sighed. She rubbed her palm against the cold marker.

"Everyone turned to look at me when Miss Green made the announcement," Corky continued. "As if I would throw a fit or storm out or something." And then she added bitterly, "As if I would care."

She kicked away a leaf that had blown onto a leg of her jeans. "I don't care anymore, Bobbi. I really don't," she said with growing emotion. "I don't know what I care about now. I just wish you were here. So that I could apologize for being mean to you the night before . . . the night before you died. I just wish you were here so you could tell me what happened."

Corky sobbed. "What happened in that shower room? Why didn't you open the door and come out? The police say you had some kind of seizure and died instantly. I was glad you didn't suffer, but I just can't understand it. Why? How did it happen? You weren't sick. You were in great shape. What happened, Bobbi? What happened?"

Then she was crying, big tears rolling down her cheeks, her nose running, the sound of her own cries pushed back at her by a rush of cold wind.

"I'm sorry. I'm sorry," she apologized to the silent, unanswering gravestone. "I keep coming here day after day, saying the same things. It's just—just—"

Corky shoved her hand into her jeans pocket, searching for a tissue. Digging deep, she found one, balled-up. She pulled it out.

And saw something shiny fall out.

She bent down and searched the wet ground at her feet until she found it. Then she stood to examine it.

Kimmy's megaphone pendant.

She had found it that day. On the locker-room floor. Near Bobbi's clothes.

On that horrible day.

She had tucked it into her jeans pocket, forgotten all about it.

As she stared at it, watching it gleam in the cold, white moonlight, Corky realized that here was a clue.

Here in her trembling hand.

Kimmy had been there. Kimmy had been in the locker room. Had been near Bobbi's things.

"Oh, no," Corky said aloud, squeezing the pendant tight in her fist. "Oh, no. Oh, no."

Did Kimmy have something to do with Bobbi's death? No one had more motive, Corky realized.

No one resented Bobbi more than Kimmy.

In fact, it wasn't just resentment. It was hatred.

Open hatred.

Kimmy hated Bobbi because she was cheerleader captain. Because Chip had dropped Kimmy and asked Bobbi out. Because Bobbi was pretty and blond and talented, and Kimmy wasn't.

Because of *everything*.

"Yes, Kimmy was there," Corky said aloud. "Kimmy was there when Bobbi died, and I have the proof in my hand."

And then, without realizing it, she was running, running between the rows of graves, her boots sliding and slipping in the mud. With the pendant wrapped tightly in her fist, she was running down to the street.

And then she was home and in the car, starting it up, the engine roaring to life, the headlights cutting through the dark night air.

I have the proof. I have the proof.

And she squealed away from her house, following the curve of Fear Street, past the dark, old houses, past the trembling, nearly bare trees, and turned toward Kimmy's house.

A few minutes later, her heart pounding, the pendant still clutched tightly in her fist, she was staring up at the large, white-shingled house, the windows all lit up, a silver Volvo parked in the drive.

Kimmy's mother opened the door, surprised to see Corky there so late, unannounced. Corky rushed past her without any explanation, tore through the front hallway, swallowing hard, gasping for air, and burst into the den.

Kimmy was there with Debra and Ronnie.

"Hey—" she called out as Corky entered.

"Here," Corky screamed accusingly, unwrapped her fist, and thrust the silver megaphone pendant into Kimmy's face.

Kimmy started, and her eyes grew wide with surprise.

Chapter 21

Kimmy's Surprise

"It's my proof!" Corky cried.

Ronnie jumped to her feet. Debra stared up at Corky from the floor, a notebook in her lap.

"My proof!" Corky repeated, holding the pendant in front of Kimmy's startled face.

"Where'd you get it?" Kimmy asked, locking her eyes onto Corky's.

"You left it somewhere," Corky said, shaking all over from her anger.

"Huh?"

"You left it somewhere, and now it's my proof!" Corky exclaimed.

"Corky—are you okay?" Ronnie asked, moving over to her and putting a hand gently on her trembling shoulder.

"You'd better sit down," Debra said, closing her notebook. "You don't look very well."

Corky pulled away from Ronnie's hand. "You were there. You were there when Bobbi died," she snarled, staring accusingly at Kimmy.

Kimmy's mouth dropped open, but she didn't reply.

"Here's my proof," Corky said, waving the pendant in Kimmy's face.

"Listen to Debra," Kimmy said finally. "Sit down." She pointed to the couch. "You're not making any sense, Corky."

"I found this in the locker room," Corky said, ignoring Kimmy's words. "On the day Bobbi died. I found it on the floor. I found it."

"Corky—please!" Kimmy insisted. "Sit down. Let me get you something hot to drink. You're shaking like a leaf!"

"Don't change the subject!" Corky screamed, realizing she was out of control, not caring, not caring at all. "I have the proof, Kimmy. I have the proof! I found your pendant under Bobbi's things."

Kimmy's expression changed from surprise to concern. "Corky," she said softly, "that pendant isn't mine."

Chapter 22

Jennifer's Surprise

"Huh?"

Corky took a step back, her expression one of suspicion and disbelief.

"It isn't mine anymore," Kimmy said, her eyes on the pendant.

"But—but—"

"I gave it to Jennifer," Kimmy said.

"She's telling the truth," Debra said quickly. Holding her notebook, she climbed to her feet and stepped up beside Kimmy, as if taking sides. Ronnie had moved back to the window and was leaning against the ledge, a troubled look on her face.

"Jennifer?" Corky asked weakly, suddenly feeling as if she were falling, falling down a dark, endless hole.

"I gave it to Jennifer. About a month ago," Kimmy said, resting her hands on her hips. "She was always telling me how much she liked it. So one day I saw her in the hall before school, and I just gave it to her."

"No," Corky insisted. "You always wore it—"

"She's telling the truth," Debra insisted. "I was there when Kimmy gave it to Jennifer. Jennifer was really happy."

"I was tired of it anyway," Kimmy said with a shrug. "The clasp was loose. It was always falling off."

Corky stared hard into Kimmy's eyes. She was telling the truth, Corky realized.

But that meant . . .

"You *hated* my sister!" Corky declared, unwilling to let Kimmy off the hook.

Kimmy shook her head. She turned her eyes to the window. "I didn't like her very much, Corky. But I didn't hate her. I guess I resented her a lot. I guess I was a little jealous of her."

"A *little?*" Corky cried.

"Okay, okay. A lot," Kimmy admitted. "But I'm not a murderer! I wouldn't kill someone because of cheerleading!"

"Jennifer—" Corky stammered.

"Jennifer isn't a killer either," Kimmy said softly. She shook her head. "You know that, Corky. Poor Jennifer—"

"But the pendant—" Corky said, staring down at it in her hand.

"Jennifer must have dropped it," Kimmy replied. "Just like I always did. I told you, the clasp was loose."

Corky's mind whirred crazily from thought to thought. She stared at the pendant as if hypnotized by it. The room started to tilt, then spin. Once again she felt as if she were falling, falling down a bottomless, dark pit.

"Corky—!" Kimmy grabbed her arm.

"Jennifer couldn't change her clothes in the locker room," Corky said, closing her eyes, trying to make the room stop spinning, trying to make the falling sensation stop. "Jennifer always changed at home. She wouldn't go in the locker room."

"Yeah. Maybe," Kimmy agreed. "But, Corky—"

"Why would Jennifer go in the locker room? Why? What was she doing there?" Corky screamed.

"Corky—stop! You're not thinking clearly!" Kimmy cried.

"Sit down," Ronnie said from across the room. "Somebody make her sit down."

"Maybe we should call her parents," Debra said at the same time.

"No!" Corky screamed, pulling out of Kimmy's grasp. "No! I have to talk to Jennifer! I *have* to! I have to know the truth!"

"Corky—please—let us call your parents," Kimmy pleaded.

But Corky had already run out of the den and was making her way down the front hallway. The three girls called to her, begging her to come back.

"What on earth is going on?" Kimmy's mom cried, poking her head out of the living room.

Corky flew past her—and out into the dark, cool night.

"Corky—come back! Come back!"

"Come back and talk!"

She ignored their pleas, their frantic, high-pitched shouts.

The car started quickly. The lights shot on. And she headed the car toward Jennifer's house in North Hills.

Past houses darkened for the night. Past empty yards and woods filled with silent, bending trees. Past Shadyside High, dark except for the spotlight out front, throwing a shimmering cone of light onto the front doors.

Jennifer's house was on a side street just north of the school. As Corky turned the corner, her headlights swept over the low ranch-style house. She braked hard, slowing the car down the street from the house, and stared across the smooth lawn.

Dark.

All the windows were dark, the shades drawn, curtains pulled.

Corky glanced at the dashboard clock. Eleven o'clock.

"Guess they all go to bed early," she said out loud.

And then she saw the headlights of a car parked at the curb in front of Jennifer's house flash on.

It was a red Skylark, Corky saw.

The car pulled slowly away from the curb and edged into the driveway to turn around. The interior lights came on for a second, and the girl in the car was illuminated.

It's Jennifer! Corky saw, her mouth dropping open.

I didn't know she could drive.

I didn't think she could move her legs enough to push the pedals.

She watched her pull the car halfway up the drive, then back up into the street, then pull off in the other direction.

Jennifer's headlights filled Corky's car with blinding white light. She's coming right at me, Corky thought. She'll see me.

Corky ducked her head, covered her face with the sleeve of her coat.

Jennifer didn't seem to notice her. The Skylark rolled slowly past, then turned right, heading toward the school.

Where could Jennifer be going by herself at eleven o'clock at night? Corky wondered.

Deciding to follow her, she eased the car into Jennifer's driveway and turned around just as Jennifer had done. Then she floored the gas pedal and shot around the corner, eager to catch up.

Racing down Park Drive, Corky quickly saw that their cars were the only two on the road. She slowed down, deciding to keep at least a block between her car and Jennifer's.

Where is she going? Where?

The question repeated and repeated in her mind.

The full moon floated at the top of the windshield, as if leading the way. A raccoon scooted into the road, hesitated in Corky's headlights, then just made it safely to the other side as Corky rolled by.

As she followed a block behind the red Skylark, Corky's thoughts went back to her emotional encounter with Kimmy. Kimmy appeared to be telling the truth about the silver pendant. And she truly seemed to be concerned about Corky.

What did that mean?

Was Jennifer in the locker room the afternoon Bobbi was killed?

Bobbi and Jennifer had become best friends. There was no reason to suspect that Jennifer might have killed Bobbi. No reason at all.

So what was she doing there that afternoon?

And what was she doing *now*?

Corky followed the Skylark as it turned onto Old Mill Road. As an oncoming car shot its headlights forward, Corky could see Jennifer's shadow reflected on the back window of the little car.

She's heading for Fear Street! Corky realized.

But why?

Is she going to my house? An unexpected visit?

No. Jennifer isn't my friend. She was Bobbi's friend.

Bobbi's friend. Bobbi's friend. Bobbi's friend.

The words repeated until they didn't make any sense.

Nothing made any sense.

She followed Jennifer's car as it turned onto Fear Street. Past the sprawling, ramshackle old houses. Past the burnt-out ruins of the old Simon Fear mansion high on its sloping, weed-covered lawn.

And then suddenly, after Fear Street curved into the thick woods, Corky saw Jennifer pull her car to the side of the road. Her headlights dimmed, then went out.

Corky hit the brakes, her car sliding to a stop less than a block behind. Quickly she cut her lights.

Corky wondered, Why is she stopping here?

Leaning forward to get a better view through the windshield, she saw where Jennifer had stopped.

The cemetery. The Fear Street cemetery.

Squinting through the darkness, she saw Jennifer's car door swing open. Saw Jennifer's hand on the door handle, pushing the door open, holding it open.

Then she saw Jennifer turn and put her feet down on the pavement.

"Oh, I don't *believe* it!" Corky muttered to herself as Jennifer pulled herself to her feet.

Stood up.

Stepped away from the car. Slammed the door. Walked onto the grass of the cemetery.

Walked.

"I don't believe it," Corky repeated, gaping at the slender, dark figure disappearing behind the gravestones.

"She walks. She can walk. Bobbi was right. That night in front of Jennifer's house. Bobbi was right. And I thought she was crazy."

Corky leapt out of the car, closing the door silently behind her. Then she began jogging along the curb, running as quietly as she could, staying in the shadows thrown by the tall trees.

She stopped and knelt behind a gnarled old oak, and peered where Jennifer had gone.

Wisps of fog floated over the graveyard. The moonlight filtering through the fog tinged everything with a pale, sickly green. Shadows shifted and shimmered in the eerie green light. The jagged tombstones glowed.

As Corky leaned against the cold, damp tree trunk, peering intently into the dimly lit scene, Jennifer reemerged. Dancing.

Dancing a strange, silent dance.

149

Her arms over her head, her legs—those legs every-one believed to be paralyzed—twirled and kicked. A silent, cheerless tango.

She was wearing her cheerleader costume. The short skirt flew up as she spun. Her dark hair flew behind her as if alive.

And what was that she was waving in her hand?

Corky squinted into the misty green light.

It was the pennant. The Shadyside pennant they had made for her after the accident. The crippling accident.

And now here was Jennifer, twirling wildly in the green moonlight. Kicking and twirling. Waving the pennant high.

Dancing in a narrow circle. Bending her back, raising her face to the moon, her long hair flowing down nearly to the ground.

Round and round.

Around a tombstone, Corky realized.

Jennifer was circling a tall tombstone, surrounded by four other stones.

Sarah Fear's tombstone.

Waving the pennant, she kicked her legs high as if leading a silent parade. Then, once again, she arched her back, raising her face to the moon.

Her eyes closed, the pale green light played off her face. She bowed deeply, crossing her legs as she dipped, a strange curtsy to the moon. And then she rose up and began moving slowly to an unheard rhythm, twirling around the gravestone, her eyes closed, a strange, tranquil smile on her face.

Corky couldn't stand it any longer.

Pushing herself away from the tree, she lurched forward into the graveyard, her boots sinking into the wet mud.

"Jennifer—" she called, her voice sounding tiny and hollow on the wind. "Jennifer—what's going on?"

Chapter 23

"I'm Not Jennifer"

Jennifer halted her strange dance and opened her eyes. Her smile faded. She lowered the pennant to her side.

Corky ran, stopping before the first row of gravestones. "Jennifer—what are you doing?"

Jennifer's eyes reflected the green moonlight as she turned to face Corky. "I'm not Jennifer," she said, her voice husky, almost breathless.

"Huh? Jennifer—I saw you dancing," Corky cried.

"I'm not Jennifer," she repeated darkly, standing directly in front of Sarah Fear's tombstone. And then she screamed: *"I'm not Jennifer!"*

"Jennifer—I *saw* you!" Corky insisted.

As if in reply, Jennifer lifted one hand high above her head and waved it as if summoning someone.

"Oh!" Corky cried out, raising her hands to her face

as the grass flew off Sarah Fear's grave, and the dirt began to rise.

Jennifer waved her hand high above her head, and the dirt rose up like a dark curtain, flying off the grave, flying high into the black sky.

And then the dirt was swirling around them both, thicker and thicker, until Corky couldn't see beyond it, until Corky was forced to move closer to Jennifer.

Faster and faster the curtain of dirt swirled, until it became a raging, dark whirlwind, like a tornado funnel.

Covering her eyes with her arm, Corky staggered forward, forward—until she was standing face-to-face with Jennifer. Jennifer held her hand high as if directing the swirling dirt, her eyes aglow with excitement, the excitement of her power.

"Jennifer—what are you doing? Stop it! Stop it— *please!*"

Corky's frightened plea was drowned out by the roar of the spinning dirt. The roar drowned out all sound, all thoughts. She could no longer see the moon or the sky, the graves, the trees.

Inside the dark funnel of dirt, she could see only Jennifer. Jennifer, her eyes glowing with an eerie green light, glaring at Corky, her expression hard, angry, her hand still raised high over her head.

They were alone, the two of them, trapped inside this frightening storm of graveyard dirt.

And then the roar faded and died as the dirt continued to whirl around them. And Jennifer's throaty voice, a voice Corky had never heard before, rose in the fresh silence. "I am not Jennifer," she repeated, glaring coldly at Corky. "Jennifer is dead. Jennifer died weeks ago."

"What are you saying?" Corky cried, wrapping her arms around herself as if for protection. "What is *happening?*"

"Jennifer died in the bus accident," the husky voice revealed, her eyes lighting up, as if the words were giving her pleasure. "She was dead that night in the rain. She died on top of Sarah Fear's grave."

"Jennifer—what are you *saying?*" Corky cried. Her eyes darted around, searching for an escape route. But the swirling black column of dirt offered no hope of escape.

"I waited so long, so long," the husky voice said, deepening with sudden sadness. "I waited so long—and then Jennifer came along. . . ."

"I don't understand," Corky started. "I don't—"

"Buried for so long," the voice continued. "Buried down there for a hundred years with Sarah Fear. Waiting. Waiting."

"You're—you're *Sarah Fear?*" Corky stammered, staring into the angry, glowing eyes.

"Not anymore," came the reply.

Corky shuddered and hugged herself tightly.

This isn't happening.

The heavy funnel of dirt from the grave continued to swirl silently around the two girls, blocking out all sound, all light, all evidence that the rest of the world existed.

"I—I don't get it," Corky stammered. "Are you some kind of ghost? An evil spirit?"

Again Jennifer threw back her head in laughter. "That is a quaint way of putting it," she replied, sneering. She pointed down to the grave. "Nearly a hundred years I waited down there for a new body. And then Jennifer came along."

"Please—" Corky cried, lowering her hands to her sides. "Stop. Let me go now, okay?"

Jennifer shook her head, her eyes lighting up with pleasure.

"No—please," Corky begged. "Let me go. What do you want with me?"

A thin smile played over Jennifer's lips. "It's *your* turn to go down there," she said, pointing into the grave.

Chapter 24

Into the Coffin

"No!" Corky tried to back away. But she was trapped, trapped inside the spinning dirt as thick as a garden wall.

Jennifer leaned forward until her eyes burned so close to Corky that she could feel their heat. "Nearly a hundred years I waited. But now I'm alive inside Jennifer, and Jennifer's enemies will pay." Again she pointed down into the grave. "Now it's your turn, Corky."

"But why?" Corky cried. "I haven't done anything to you."

"Haven't *done* anything? You and your sister—with your perfect faces? Your perfect bodies? Your perfect lives?"

"But—" Corky turned her head, tried to get away from the searing heat of the evil, burning eyes.

A bitter smile formed on Jennifer's eerily glowing face. "But I showed Bobbi. I showed Bobbi and that boy, Chip."

"You frightened them," Corky said, realizing what had happened, realizing that her sister's wild stories were all true. "You paralyzed them. And then—you killed Bobbi," Corky said, choking out the words.

Jennifer nodded once and locked her eyes on Corky. "Now it's your turn."

"No! Jennifer—*wait!*" Corky screamed.

The evil spirit inside Jennifer's body laughed scornfully. She pointed at her feet. "Look down there, Corky dear. Look down at your new home."

Corky, too frightened to disobey, turned her eyes down.

With another wave of Jennifer's hand, more dirt flew up into the swirling dirt funnel. As the dirt rose up in eerie silence, Corky stared down into a deep hole. To her horror, the hole revealed the top of a coffin, the dark wood swollen and warped.

"See your new home—and your new friend!" the evil spirit cried in its hoarse, dead voice.

"Oh!" Corky moaned weakly as the coffin lid creaked open.

Still compelled to peer down into the darkness, Corky watched the lid lift all the way up.

Inside the coffin, she saw a rotting skeleton, its eyeless skull staring up at her with a toothy grin.

The skeleton was moving. Quivering all over.

No.

Staring hard, unable to remove her eyes from the ghastly sight, Corky saw why the skeleton appeared to quiver.

Those were worms moving on the bones, thousands of white worms slithering over the skeleton, crawling over the rotting remains of Sarah Fear.

"Oh!" Corky felt her stomach heave, felt her throat tighten in disgust.

She shut her eyes and turned away, but the sight of the thousands of slithering white worms stayed with her.

Swallowing hard, trying to shake away the horrifying picture, she suddenly heard voices. Far away yet familiar.

For a brief, terrifying moment, she thought it was the voice of Sarah Fear, calling to her from down in the open grave.

But then she recognized Kimmy's voice. And heard Debra's reply. And Ronnie's frightened shout.

The voices sounded far away because they came from outside the wall of dirt.

They must have followed me, Corky realized.

"Your friends are too late to save you," Jennifer said calmly, without urgency. She raised both hands.

"No—please!" Corky screamed. "Please—don't!"

Ignoring her cries, Jennifer shoved Corky with startling strength, inhuman strength.

Still screaming, Corky toppled into the hole, down to join Sarah Fear in the open, worm-ridden coffin.

Chapter 25

Corky Loses

Down into the hole. Into the warped, swollen coffin.

Down to the white worms.

But even in her screaming terror, Corky's body responded, remembering the cheerleading skills, the moves her body had practiced over the years until they had become reflexive, a part of her.

She landed hard on her feet. Absorbed the pressure of the landing by bending her knees. Then pushed up, up—into a high standing jump. Raised her hands. Caught the top of the open grave as the wall of dirt began to swirl back down on her. Pulled herself up and out as the dirt began to lower itself back into the hole.

Panting loudly, she crawled away from the hole, away from the horror.

Jennifer had already turned away, turned around to face the three cheerleaders.

Still acting by reflex, her mind still paralyzed by the horrors of the open grave, her body forced to act on its own, Corky flung herself on Jennifer. Caught her from behind. Wrapped her arms around Jennifer's waist. Swung her back toward the open grave.

She struggled to wrestle Jennifer into the hole. Into the coffin. To wrestle the evil spirit back to where it belonged, as the dirt continued to rain down, down, down.

Jennifer cried out in her husky, deep voice, trying to pull out of Corky's desperate hug.

The pennant, which she had clutched all the while, fell from her hand. Corky watched it drop into the hole. It landed silently among the bones and worms.

They wrestled nearer to the edge of the hole. Corky pulled, pulled with all her strength, tightening her arms around Jennifer's waist, trying to throw her down.

Jennifer pulled back, crying out in protest.

Closer to the hole. Closer to the edge.

I can do it! Corky thought. I can do it!

But then Jennifer turned to face her, her eyes wild with fury. She opened her mouth wide, wider—and a wind blew out, a stench, a vapor, a wind that howled over Corky, covered her face, filled her nostrils.

Jennifer tilted her head, closed her eyes, and the vapor roared out of her, reeking of death, of decay, of all that is foul.

It blew into Corky's face, hot and wet and sour. Corky gagged and turned her face.

But the wind still howled out of Jennifer's mouth,

encircled Corky and choked her in its thick, hot stench.

I'm going to suffocate, she thought.

I can't breathe. I'm going to suffocate. The smell. The smell is too sickening!

Corky realized she was weakening, about to lose the fight.

One last tug. She held her breath and braced herself, summoned all of her remaining strength for one last tug.

Now! she told herself.

And heaved with all her might, her arms wrapped tightly around Jennifer's waist.

Into the grave! Corky thought. *Jennifer—go down into the grave!*

But Jennifer was too strong.

The foul wind raged and howled from her open mouth.

Jennifer didn't budge.

I'm lost, Corky thought.

Chapter 26

Buried

Corky felt her arms slip off Jennifer's waist.

I'm lost. I'm lost.

As the dirt rained down, she could suddenly hear the terrified cries of the three girls.

Jennifer's eyes were open wide as the sour wind howled from her mouth. She knew she had won. She knew her evil had triumphed.

First Bobbi. Now me, Corky thought.

Bobbi. Bobbi.

The thought of her sister filled her with renewed anger. With an anguished cry, Corky threw herself onto Jennifer's back and wrapped her hands around Jennifer's throat from behind.

Jennifer struggled as Corky tightened her grip, tightened her hands, began to choke Jennifer, choke the evil spirit inside Jennifer's body, pushing her head down.

162

The raging stream of foul vapor from Jennifer's mouth blew into the hole now, into the open grave. Corky could see it, blowing the worms around in the coffin.

"Yes!" she cried aloud, hearing the wind lose its howl, feeling it weaken as it poured into the coffin.

All the evil pouring down into the coffin.

And as Corky continued to choke her, Jennifer felt lighter, lighter. Light as air.

And the wind stopped. Jennifer uttered a feeble groan, and the wind stopped.

"Yes!" Corky cried, not loosening her grip on Jennifer's throat.

The evil spirit is abandoning her, Corky thought.

She could feel it leaving, could feel Jennifer's body growing light.

Corky let go.

Jennifer lay facedown in the dirt.

Corky watched as the coffin lid slammed shut, trapping the evil vapor, trapping the evil spirit inside.

The dirt rained down in a dark, thunderous avalanche, filling the hole, re-covering the grave.

Buried. The evil spirit is buried again, Corky thought, gasping in the cool, sweet air, the clean air, letting the fresh night air fill her lungs.

She realized she was still on her knees in the soft dirt.

"Corky—!" Kimmy was screaming.

The three girls were standing right in front of her, peering at the grave in horror. They had seen it all, seen every moment of Corky's desperate battle. Now they huddled around her.

"Corky—are you *okay?*" Ronnie cried.

All four of them turned their eyes to Jennifer's body. Slowly Corky rolled her over so she was face up. "Ohh," Kimmy groaned.

Ronnie gagged and held on to Debra to keep from sinking to her knees.

As the girls gaped in silent horror, Jennifer's skin dried and crumpled, flaking off in chunks. Her long hair fell off, strands blowing away in the breeze. Her eyes sank back into her skull, then rotted into dark pits. Her cheerleader costume appeared to grow larger as her flesh decayed underneath it, and her bones appeared.

Before Corky realized what was happening, she felt Kimmy's arm slide around her shoulders. "It's okay, Corky," Kimmy whispered. "You're okay now. It's all going to be okay."

And then they heard a man's voice calling from the street. "What's going on here?"

Darting beams from flashlights danced over the ground. The girls looked up into the suspicious faces of two uniformed Shadyside officers.

"What's going on here? One of the neighbors reported a—"

Both of the young officers gasped in surprise as they saw the body sprawled on the ground beside the four girls, the body draped in a cheerleader's costume.

"What on earth—?"

"It's Jennifer," Corky managed to say from the midst of her confusion. "It's Jennifer Daly. I followed her here. She—"

"Huh?" Both police directed their lights from the body to Corky's face. "You followed her here? Are you sure, miss?"

164

"Yes. I followed her here. She was dancing—"

"You didn't follow this girl, miss," the policeman said, eyeing Corky intently. "This girl hasn't been dancing tonight. Take a good look at the corpse. This girl has been dead for weeks!"

Jennifer's anguished parents, awakened and summoned to the police station, had demanded answers.

But there were no reasonable answers, no logical answers.

Corky's parents had also arrived, as upset and confused as everyone else. They had waited patiently with their daughter during the hours of questioning, the police asking the same questions again and again, dissatisfied with the answers they received from Corky and the other three girls.

"Fear Street," one of the policemen had said grimly, shaking his head. "Fear Street . . ."

A few minutes later he allowed them all to go home.

As Corky climbed the stairs to her room, the room she had shared with her sister, she thought of Bobbi.

Bobbi had died because of the evil spirit's jealousy.

And now Corky was alone. Left alone to remember forever the horrors of this night.

She turned on the light and glanced at the bedside clock. Three o'clock in the morning. Wearily, feeling numb, she tugged off her clothes, letting them fall to the floor, and pulled a nightgown over her head.

"Bobbi—I miss you so much!" she cried out loud.

Trying to force back the sobs that threatened to burst out of her throat, she turned off the light and lowered herself into bed.

Bobbi is gone forever, she told herself miserably.

But so is the evil spirit.

The evil spirit is buried once again, buried in the old grave, locked in the coffin under six feet of dirt where it can't harm anyone ever again.

She sighed, pulling the covers up to her chin.

"Hey—"

There was something in her bed.

With a startled cry, she reached down, grabbed it, held it tightly.

She clicked on the lamp and stared at it, blinking as her eyes adjusted to the light.

It was the maroon and white pennant with Jennifer's name stitched across the front.

She stared at the pennant, reading the name again and again.

Then it fell from her hand and she started to scream.

THE NIGHTMARES NEVER END . . . WHEN YOU VISIT

Next . . .
CHEERLEADERS: THE SECOND EVIL

Corky Corcoran is trying to put the nightmare of her sister Bobbi's death behind her. She's back on the Shadyside cheerleading squad and has become friends with Kimmy, Debra, and Ronnie. But just when everything seems like it's back to normal for Corky, she hears horrible screams in the gym, notices a very strange young man following her, and thinks she sees her dead sister rise from the grave. And then the murders begin again. . . .

About the Author

R. L. STINE doesn't know *where* he gets the ideas for his scary books! But he wants to assure worried readers that none of the horrors of FEAR STREET ever happened to him in real life.

Bob lives in New York City with his wife and twelve-year-old son. He is the author of more than twenty bestselling mysteries and thrillers for Young Adult readers. He also writes funny novels, joke books, and books for younger readers.

In addition to his publishing work, he is Head Writer of the children's TV show "Eureeka's Castle," seen on Nickelodeon.